GEOMETRIC REGIONAL NOVEL

Gert Jonke's Works in German

Geometrischer Heimatroman. Frankfurt: Suhrkamp, 1969.

Glashausbesichtigung. Frankfurt: Suhrkamp, 1970.

Beginn einer Verzweiflung. Salzburg: Residenz, 1970.

Musikgeschichte. Berlin: Literarisches Colloquium, 1970.

Weltbilder: 49 Beschreibungen. Edited with Leo Navratil. München: Hanser, 1970.

Die Vermehrung der Leuchttürme. Frankfurt: Suhrkamp, 1971.

Die Hinterhältigkeit der Windmaschinen oder Ein Schluck Gras Löscht jeden Durst im Inland und im Ausland auch: Tragödie in drei Akten. Frankfurt: Suhrkamp, 1972.

Im Inland und im Ausland auch: Prosa. Gedichte. Hörspiel. Theaterstück. Frankfurt: Suhrkamp, 1974.

Schule der Geläufigkeit. Frankfurt: Suhrkamp, 1977.

Der ferne Klang. Salzburg: Residenz, 1979.

Die erste Reise zum unerforschten Grund des stillen Horizonts. Salzburg: Residenz, 1980.

Erwachen zum großen Schlafkrieg. Salzburg: Residenz, 1982.

Der Kopf des Georg Friedrich Händel. Salzburg: Residenz, 1988.

Sanftwut oder Der Ohrenmaschinist. Salzburg: Residenz, 1990.

Opus 111. Ein Klavierstück. Frankfurt: Verlag der Autoren, 1993.

Stoffgewitter. Salzburg: Residenz, 1996.

Es singen die Steine: ein Stück Naturtheater. Salzburg: Residenz, 1998.

GEOMETRIC REGIONAL NOVEL

GERT JONKE

Translated with an afterword by
Johannes W. Vazulik

Dalkey Archive Press

The translator and publisher would like to thank the Austrian Federal Ministry for Education and the Arts for financial assistance toward this translation.

Originally published as *Geometrischer Heimatroman* in 1969 by Suhrkamp Verlag; a revised version appeared in the omnibus *Die erste Reise zum unerforschten Grund des stillen Horizonts,* published by Residenz Verlag in 1980. © 1980 by Residenz Verlag.

Library of Congress Cataloging-in-Publication Data:

Jonke, Gert, 1946-
        [Geometrischer Heimatroman. English]
        Geometric regional novel / Gert Jonke ; translated with an afterword by Johannes W. Vazulik. — 1st paperback ed.
        I. Title.
PT2670.05G413   1994   833'.914—dc20   93-33256
ISBN 1-56478-231-X

This publication is partially supported by grants from the National Endowment for the Arts, a federal agency, and the Illinois Arts Council, a state agency.

Dalkey Archive Press
Illinois State University
Campus Box 4241
Normal, IL 61790-4241

Visit our web site at: www.dalkeyarchive.com

Printed on permanent/durable acid-free paper and bound in the United States of America.

GEOMETRIC REGIONAL NOVEL

The Village Square

The village square is rectangular, bordering on the houses gathered around it; streets and lanes flow into it; other than the well in the center, in which the paving stone patterns seek their source and from which they spread out like rays, there is nothing in the village square.

A figure, suddenly appearing in the square, approaches the well and draws water, making the winch creak; it turns from the well, a jug on its head, vanishes into a narrow side street. Or, perhaps, at the edges, along the four lines of house facades, morning visits are being exchanged, quickly hiding behind doors, hair and shawls disappearing into door cracks.

Then at noon a few bustle about; the children leave the schoolhouse, tossing caps and satchels above the roofs, the teacher goes to the inn, the priest closes the window.

—*We can walk across the village square.*

—*Yes, let's walk across the village square.*

—*Other than the well in the center, the village square is empty.*

No, that's not true, because there are b e n c h e s set up along the edges, their backs turned toward the walls.

We had hidden in the blacksmith's workshop, cheeks pressed up against the walls; no one saw us, and you said

—*let's walk across the village square.*

—*No, let's not walk across the village square,*

I retorted, because all at once I saw p e o p l e sitting on the b e n c h e s as if suddenly put there, two on each bench.

We couldn't walk across the village square b e c a u s e   w e   w e r e n ' t
s u p p o s e d   t o   b e   s e e n .
—*Let's walk across the village square anyhow.*
—*We can't walk across the village square,*
I said once more;
meanwhile, the first figure on the first bench nearest us had risen, while the
figure sitting on the bench opposite the first bench had also risen;
then they walked toward each other, met each other on the center line dividing the village square, raised their right hands, thrust their palms toward
each other, clasped, shook them up and down, released them, turned away
from each other, went back to their benches, sat down again;
at the same time, the second figure sitting on the first bench nearest us had
risen, while the second figure sitting on the bench opposite the first bench
had also risen; then they walked toward each other . . .

                                                                    . . . until all
figures sitting opposite each other on opposite benches had risen, walked
toward each other, shaken hands, walked back to their respective benches,
and sat down again.
We couldn't walk across the village square because we weren't supposed to
be seen by the figures sitting on the benches, rising, walking toward each
other, shaking hands, turning away from each other, sitting down again; we
had hidden in the blacksmith's workshop, cheeks pressed up against the
walls; no one saw us,
and that's the way w e   observed how the people sitting on the benches
c o u l d n ' t   see us because we didn't walk across the village square;
yes, we saw
how they d i d n ' t   see us.

The Village

The village lies in a hollow.

It is surrounded by mountains.

The silhouetted margin of the mountain range north of the village has the shape of four curves that lead into one another:

a sine curve, a cosine curve, and a sine and a cosine curve, each displaced by one and three-quarter phases.

The mountain range south of the village is a jagged limestone ridge, whose silhouetted margin is comparable to the diagram of a repeatedly interrupted energy flow.

The mountain range east of the village has foothill-like features.

It is most convenient to approach the village from the east because the roads across those mountains are well maintained, marked, signposted, and identified; only a few boulders that have fallen onto the roads delay the progress of your journey; a relatively few potholes may also cause you to stumble.

Signs are posted along the roadsides every hundred meters.

CAUTION

IN CASE OF SNOW AND ICE, TRAVEL IN THIS AREA IS RESTRICTED TO S A N D E D ROADS SLIDING ON THE ICE, SLEIGHING, AND SKIING ARE PROHIBITED.

There are warning signs and road condition notices:

IN CASE OF SNOW AND ICE,

THIS ROAD IS NOT CLEARED OR SANDED

PROCEED AT YOUR O W N R I S K .

The roads into the village are bounded by verdigris-covered pasture fences, whose rectangular patterns partition the countryside.

It's a good thing that the roads are protected by fences, because this makes it more difficult for the b u l l s , whose dark skins sprinkle the area with brown spots, to hinder the person who wants to hike to the village. This way, hikers don't have to keep running away from bulls but can calmly leave their pistols packed in their knapsacks and comfortably fasten their sabers on their backs.

Only now and then does a bull stand behind the fence at the road and bellow at you, who wants to get to the village. The bull would like to go over the fence, but it can't. The fence prevents it from molesting you, you can safely continue on your way to the village. To be sure, the bull behind the fence will accompany you for a while, the two of you will cover a part of your shared way separated from each other by a fence; the bull will attempt to push the fence aside with its horns but, most of the time, will be too weak to break through it. However, should the bull locate a weak spot in the fence and break through it, with the evil thought,

just wait, I'll get you yet,

then you should not lose your composure because of the bull's wicked thoughts, which you suddenly discover; you will have no choice but to run, to dodge and outwit the bull with your cunning. The hiker will attempt to unfasten the saber from his back, to take the knapsack from his back, to get the pistol out of the knapsack.

If he succeeds, he'll have an easy time of it.

While brandishing his saber in front of the bull, he releases the safety catch of his pistol.

If one succeeds in piercing the bull the way bullfighters do, without having to use the pistol, one can say in the evening

—you did well today because you saved a bullet.

However, if the hiker does not succeed in killing the bull with the saber, use of the firearm is definitely recommended.

If he hits the bull in the brain, he doesn't need to keep on shooting and he can save all subsequent bullets. To be sure, the bull will continue to charge at you furiously, but a few seconds later it will collapse and die.

However, should the hiker hit the bull only in a leg or in the testicles, it is recommended that the bull also be shot in the brain as it is lying collapsed on the road and in its death throes is kicking up its legs. By no means should the hiker spare his feeling of pity, but should put his pistol to the bull's forehead; he need not fear that the bull will injure, bother, or interrupt him; rather it will hold out its head patiently toward him, turn its forehead or temple to the muzzle of the pistol, and wait for the coup de grace.

As a rule, however, your motto should be:

Better two shots in the brain than none at all.

The very strict Animal Protective League officiating in the village will be especially thankful to you for it.

Should the hiker be uncertain of actually having hit the bull in the brain, or should it only appear that he has hit the bull in the brain, whereas, in reality, perhaps he hasn't hit the bull in the brain at all, he only fancies having hit the bull in the brain, but this isn't the case at all, then he should shoot it in the brain a second time, then he can stop in the village feeling confident and cheerful.

If the hiker on the way to the village has finished off a bull, it is his d u t y t o r e p o r t the circumstances i n t h e v i l l a g e , whereupon a group of men will gather there and set out for the designated site in the countryside to transport the bull to the village.

The bull is then skewered and roasted in the village square.

Everyone receives a piece of roasted meat. The hiker will also get one.

The animal's testicles, however, are reserved for the mayor, are always handed over to his maid, who takes them to the kitchen of the town hall, hands them over to the mayor's cook, who fries them with rare herbs in hot fat and serves them to the mayor.

When the mayor has eaten the bull's testicles, he goes out onto the village square, where the rest of the bull, skewered over the fire, is being turned.

It is the mayor's custom to eat a piece of meat together with the people of the village. Some say, however, that the mayor does this less for culinary reasons than for psychological ones. He is said to cultivate a certain popularity with the people of the village by eating with them. During the meal the problems of the village are discussed. The mayor hears from his people about the problems of the village and acts accordingly. They say that the mayor uses psychology. He is a good psychologist, they claim. He practices affability. In private some whisper that when he was young he studied economic theory for two semesters in the city. Thereafter, he allegedly became feebleminded. But that isn't known for sure. It is also possible, however, that such things are only said so that no one will believe them. Thus, it is a moot point whether the mayor is or is not feebleminded:

some say that he is, that this is proven by the very fact that one would want to conceal it by allowing such a rumor to circulate, which is only supposed to circulate so that no one would believe it or think it possible; that's how they want to conceal the mayor's feeblemindedness, because this party maintains, not at all incorrectly, that an unbelievable truth can only be made unbelievable in turn by the same unbelievable truth;

that's how the intellectuals in the village talk, for the most part;

the others say, impossible that the mayor is feebleminded, because the rumor is only a malicious ploy by those who want to hurt the mayor because they envy him his high and honorable position and want to detract from the good he has done for the village.

But people don't like to talk about it, unless concealed, in secret, and then always behind the protective walls of barns. Because politics, as is known even in the village, has always been a hot potato.

As soon as the mayor has eaten two pieces of roasted bull's meat with his people, he withdraws into the town hall. Before disappearing behind the town hall door, he waves his right hand and smiles to the people of the village.

Then the door of the town hall closes behind him.

The villagers then consume the rest of the bull. After the meal the dogs and cats also get their share. Later, the animal's skeleton is buried north of the village behind the cemetery wall.

The following day, you can see black circles on the white limestone pavement of the village square, the traces of charcoal; the odor of burnt wood and tallow still hangs in the air, the tanning odor of hides stretched out to dry in the yards and shaking in the wind.

But, it is also possible
that no hide is shaking in the wind, no cattle hides are being stretched out

to dry in the yards, neither tanning odor nor odor of burnt tallow nor of
burnt wood is noticeable in the air, no charcoal traces are visible, you
can't see a single black circle on the white limestone pavement of the vil-
lage square;
it is possible
that no bull's skeleton is buried north of the village behind the cemetery
wall, the dogs and cats get no share, the meal is not concluded, the people
of the village do not consume the rest of the bull, the door of the town hall
does not close behind the mayor, he neither smiles nor waves to the people
of the village, does not disappear behind the door of the town hall;
it is possible
that the mayor does not withdraw again into the town hall, has not eaten
two pieces of roasted bull's meat with his people, does not practice affabil-
ity, is not a good psychologist, does not use psychology, the mayor does not
in any way hear about the problems of the village from his people, nor
does he act accordingly, during the meal the problems of the village are
not discussed, the mayor does not cultivate a certain popularity by shar-
ing a meal with the people, thus, does not use psychology, does not have an
opportunity to practice this for purely culinary reasons, the mayor does
not eat meat together with the people, the rest of the bull is neither turned
over the fire nor skewered;
it is entirely possible
that the mayor does not go out onto the village square, does not eat the
bull's testicles, the cook in the town hall does not serve them to the mayor,
does not fry them with rare herbs in hot fat, the mayor's maid neither
hands the bull's testicles over to the cook nor brings them into the town
hall, the bull's testicles are not handed over to the mayor's maid, that no
testicles can be reserved for the mayor;
it is possible
that the hiker is not given a piece of meat, no one receives a piece of
roasted bull's meat, the bull is neither roasted in the village square nor
skewered, no one transports the bull into the village, no one sets out for the
designated site in the countryside, no group of men gathers, the hiker does
not report that he killed a bull on the way to the village,
for the simple reason

that he, the biker, cannot report it in the village at all because he, the
biker, did not kill the bull at all, but, on the contrary, it, the b u l l, killed
h i m,
the biker.

The countryside is divided into rectangles. The sides of the rectangles are
fences. A rectangle may be one hundred meters in length but between fifty
and seventy meters in width. There are smaller and larger rectangles as well.
Green and with brown edges. The fences are covered with verdigris.
In the west, too, the village is separated from other parts of the land by a
mountain range. The silhouetted margin of the mountain range in the west
approximates the shape of the outline of an elongated trapezoid.

> nonetheless a regular epidemic later developed in the region and the
> fences stood beside the leaves beside the branches beside the boughs
> beside the tree trunks stems blossoms bushes herds ships skiffs
> bridges fences wherever one went and it was impossible to move from
> one geometrically surveyed place to another because there were only
> fences wherever one trod wherever one went a regular epidemic in the
> land then and nothing else

The Village Square

—The village square is empty.
—We can walk across the village square.
—Other than the well, there is nothing in the village square.
—The shadows of the houses cover the stone.
—By noon the shadows are gone.
—The stone on the ground begins to glisten in the sun.
—Yes, you can hear the steps on it, the rhythm of varying gaits.
—Let's walk across the village square.
—The village square is empty.

No, that's not true, because t r e e s have been planted, trees years old, with thick trunks; carvings have been made in the bark with knives: names, numbers, square, three, Anton, ten, circle, Ludwig, triangle, Paula, five, trapezoid, seventy-two, Hans, heart, arrow.

Signs are affixed to the trunks; on them the following notice can be read:

DANGER

DURING STORMY CONDITIONS

STAND UNDER TREES AT YOUR OWN RISK

SECTION 42, MUNICIPAL DEPARTMENT OF PARKS.

The trees cast their shadows on the stone, which on mornings is moist from the dew that drips from the leaves; foliage lies on the ground, is being precisely distributed over the surface of the square by the wind, whereby it becomes necessary to sweep, clean, rid the square of leaves, whereby it has become necessary to hire someone who sweeps leaves.

I see a stranger walking toward the town hall.

He opens the door and disappears into the building.

Through the open window of the office on the second floor I see and hear him talking with the mayor. The stranger says

—*ain't ya got no work fer me?*

The mayor immediately answers

—*the village square has to be swept.*

The Artist's Performance

It is said to have happened for the first time that an artist or acrobat, or whatever such a man should be called, came into the village. People say the man rode neither on a horse, nor on an ass, nor on a mule, nor on any cattle, nor on any other pack animal of any kind, be it camel, dromedary, llama, or elephant; neither did he travel on any kind of animal-drawn wagon, nor was he carried in a sedan chair, but came into the village on foot, the usual way; three people, two assistants and a drummer, as it later turned out, supposedly accompanied him.

yes i remember earlier i heard a hissing in the air then behind us the sound of a drum rolled down the hill i turned around and saw the artist as he entered the village the two assistants behind him the drummer in front the two assistants were carrying a crate one also a folded tent then on the meadow behind us they pitched the tent it is black if you look inside you can see the wooden supports and poles with deeply carved ornaments notches grooves whose shadows let the wood appear rain-soaked upon your retina then later i again heard the sound of the drum in the narrow streets between the walls i saw the drummer walk up and down while the artist and the two assistants had long since entered the village square put down the crate opened it out came a rope up two trees standing opposite each other each at the same time with an end of the rope then up there they fastened the ends of the rope to the highest strongest limbs stretched tightened tensed the rope if you look up quite a few meters above the well you can see a distinct crack dividing the sky the black line it trembles in the air

behind the walls in the yards the people had planted shrubs in the narrow streets the doors opened halfway in the door cracks heads and pairs of eyes appeared through the slits of the door cracks i was able to divine the interior of the houses and yards

fire

shrub

fans

then the

door wings clapped shut and the drummer finished his march a little later the doors opened again and the people flocked out of the walls with kith and kin filled the streets went to the village square took position in a circle on the edges of the square

The artist or acrobat, or whatever such a man should be called, performed a great variety of artistic feats for the people gathered in the village square. To begin, the man is said to have pressed an iron rod into the hands of his two assistants; both assistants are claimed to have held the rod on the ends at chest height; the man stepped back, hands extended horizontally to the front, is said to have run toward the iron rod, hands extended horizontally to the front, until he touched the rod with his palms, then pressed vigorously; but the two are said to have braced themselves for that, whereupon the man is said to have pressed, pushed even more vigorously, whereupon, according to the accounts of the people, the rod bent.

(-flattened rolls
until they hang exactly like strings on
the horizon

i am the tightrope artist)

Fig. 1 The Artist's Tent

The people are said to have stood there quite astonished at first, but were finally induced to friendly bursts of applause, whereupon the man, the artist or acrobat, or whatever someone like that should be called, supposedly bowed.

A man is said to have circulated among the people with a tin plate, putting the plate under their noses, whereupon the people allegedly reached into their coat pockets, took out coins, and tossed them into the plate; the coins are said to have clattered on the tin.

yes i remember you said
—*i suppose we'll have to wait for the night listen as he with his assistants and drummer leaves the inn very late the steps on the pavement the steps in the grass they'll probably also light the lamp hang it in front of the tent who knows they might forget to put the lamp out and its glow will creep into the faces of our sleep*
you said
—*i suppose we'll have to wait until the lamp goes out by itself*

Then the showman is said to have taken a chain, girded his chest, taken a deep breath, expanded his chest, quite obviously attempting to break the chain by expanding his chest, at which he apparently was not immediately successful, whereupon he took another deep breath and expanded his chest again; and thereupon, or as is claimed, the chain did finally burst in two and fall clanking to the ground, whereupon the people applauded enthusiastically and the man bowed benevolently. The artist's performance is said to have been judged very favorably by the people of the village,
sound work, respectable accomplishment, honest and decent, not the usual tricks, at least you know what you're getting, you don't get taken.
All kinds of opinions could be heard,
knows his business, knows what he wants, that sort of thing is rare today, one should have nerves like that, a fine fellow, a holder of distinguished service crosses first and second class.
A man is said to have circulated among the people with a tin plate and put the plate under the people's noses,
might take in quite a bit, but the risk, if anything ever goes awry, no fireman will pull him out, he'll have to see for himself how to get out of it, in that kind of a fix you're on your own.
The people are said to have reached into their coat pockets, taken out coins, and tossed them into the plate, because coins could be heard to clatter on the tin,
the risk that something might go wrong one day, and something always goes wrong, sooner or later.
Then the artist is said to have taken out a large coil, fastened it on the ground, took hold of the upper end of the coil between his teeth, pulled with his teeth, his face distorted, pulled with his teeth, his face distorted, pulled with his teeth until the stretched-out coil finally broke, whereupon, it is reported, the people applauded loudly, and the artist or acrobat, or whatever one should call him, bowed. On the other hand, or so they say, quite a few people judged the artist's performance very negatively,
old hat, leaves me cold, the usual tricks, knows his customers, nothing new to offer.
All kinds of opinions could be heard,
know how it's done, best to do it in such a way, you see, that no one notices

anything, no better than the others, nobody pulls a fast one on me, seen too much, drifter, good-for-nothing clown, whoremonger and flophouse sweeper, crusader forsaken by Christ and all mankind, a Godseeker wandering about the countryside.

A man is said to have circulated among the people with a tin plate and put the plate under the people's noses,

might take in quite a bit, but everything ends up with the innkeeper, you can bet on that.

The people are said to have reached into their coat pockets, taken out coins, and tossed them into the plate; one heard the coins clatter on the tin, *these people drink a lot, need it too, but one drop over the limit, then it's better not to go near them, this sort of people turns nasty quickly, you know.*

For the finale the man is said to have performed a tightrope walk.

He climbed up one tree and positioned himself on the rope whose ends had been fastened on the highest strongest limbs of two trees standing opposite each other.

yes i remember
—*positions himself on the black line in the sky*
—*hands extended horizontally at his sides*
—*begins to walk across the sky*
—*advances*
—*puts one foot in front of the other*
—*bound and determined*
—*holds on to the barely discernible transparent cracks in the walls of air whose pattern of trembling streaks is blurred by the light*
—*the edges of the walls are round i say*
—*the people have the backs of their heads pressed up against their backs*
—*the limb no the limb is swaying*
—*the black line that is supporting the cloud walker*
—*if only he would reach the aerial position above the well and geometrically perpendicular to it*
—*halfway is almost the whole way*

—the people are tensely silent with open mouths
—he'll make it i say
—right puts one foot in front of the other
—bound and determined
—further along the transparent walls of air
—the edges of the walls are round
—the limb no the limb is swaying
—the leaves on the limb they are being moved by the wind
—no there is no wind at all they are being moved by the swaying of the limb which sags again and again under the strain from the end of the rope fastened to it
—no isn't swaying
—yes is swaying
—impossible unthinkable the consequences
—the people have the backs of their heads pressed up against their backs
—the black line is swaying more vigorously
—the dark crack that cuts the sky in two
—the leaves on the limb they are being moved by the wind
—no by the rope that's being overloaded by the weight of the cloud walker
—has now reached the aerial position exactly above the well and geometrically perpendicular to it
—half of the way behind him that's the main thing
—in the white air
—the limb no

Suddenly, it is reported, people then had to witness how the limb broke, how the rope under his soles, under his feet, slipped downward, gave way, but he, nonetheless, h e l d   t i g h t l y   o n   t o   t h e   t r a n s p a r e n t s k y , his fingers clawed into the cracks, chinks, gaps in the walls of air, climbed upwards into the transparent sky, although the rope evidently must have fallen away beneath him; yes, he is said to have c l i m b e d t h r o u g h   t h e   t r e m b l i n g   s t r e a k s until somewhat further up he reached the top of the first wall of air, is said to have climbed over it and disappeared in the transparent white sky.

According to other reports, of course, he is said to have fallen down along with the rope, and in such an unfortunate way that his back landed on the crossbar of the well winch and his body lay motionless and broken above the well, whereupon a few people are said to have screamed like mad, while others threw their hats in the air or reached into their coat pockets, taking out the rest of their coins and tossing them into the center of the square; they say a lot of money was collected, probably for the funeral, and the assistants allegedly began the cleanup work; they really had to, things could not have been left like that, it is supposed to have looked downright indecent.

yes i remember later then the people again withdrew into the walls with kith and kin disappeared between the door cracks through the slits of the door cracks i was able to divine the interior of the houses and yards
   fire
    shrub
     fans
      then i believed having heard another hissing in the air
    fur
     button
      wedge
       which rolled down the other side of the hill behind us
    hair
     window
      wood
       moving farther and farther away
  joints
   shadows
    pavement
     i turned around
       pond
        chimney

pattern
      and saw nothing
            crest
                fence
                    sign

(It will be best if we keep to the objective and factual report of the press.)

Regrettably, all too often, access to the public is facilitated for so-called "artists," who, being reckless agitators and imitators in the service of radical Left machinations, then have to conceal their dilettantism and their lack of ability under the shoddy pretext of an allegedly "modern trend." This time, however, we were dealing with a master who must be taken seriously and who was outstanding in his ability to interpret the ups and downs of moods in the various stages of life, an interpretation as joyful and life-affirming, friendly and outgoing, high-spirited and expressive, as it was driven by a towering sense of mission, of moving spiritual engagement, profound earnestness, purest serenity, and unparalleled inner composure.

The drummer had walked through the narrow streets to gather the people. The people stood in a circle in the village square.

To begin, the artist gave a small sample of his ability. He had his two assistants take position and gave them a thick iron rod, whose ends they held at chest height. Then the artist went back about five steps and dashed with such suddenness and unbelievable ferocity toward the rod—no one would have thought it remotely possible—the rod was bent completely out of shape. The people were enthusiastic and applauded vigorously. The technical perfection and elegance of the artist received general admiration and lively comment. The two able assistants, without whose trustworthy steadfastness the first item on the program could not have succeeded, also deserve favorable mention. The two upright lads proved their mettle; they really have to be strong, or the artist undoubtedly would have flung them and the rod through the audience and against the nearest house.

For the next item on the program the artist took a chain, wrapped it around his chest, and, urged on by the crescendo of the drum roll, expanded the latter in such a powerful way that—no one would have thought it possible—a link of the chain burst, the chain let go of his chest and fell rattling to the ground. The audience responded with hearty applause. Special admiration, as well as lively discussion and comment, were elicited by the sparkling vitality of the artist; it was the general consensus that he was a master in his field. For the next item on his program the artist took a large thick coil, fastened it to the ground, put the upper end of the coil between his teeth, and pulled on it with his teeth so tenaciously and vigorously that—no one would have thought it possible—the coil was pulled apart. The audience was thrilled, there was vigorous clapping and enthusiastic applause. General admiration, discussion, and comment were also elicited by the artist's great empathy, as well as the versatility of the repertoire he has in stock. One can do naught but proclaim: Well done, indeed!

Our master, who, throughout the entire truly comprehensive program, was really in excellent form, proved completely capable of giving his wide-ranging yet solid offerings a cloak of mysticism and of manifesting transfiguration and purification so that it was obvious to all that here was a man who, because of his acquired maturity, has achieved his expertise fair and square, by hard work and unflagging industry.

The high point and conclusion of the program consisted of the so-called "tightrope walk." The two able assistants, even before the start of the performance, had stretched a rope from the top of a tree across the village square to the top of a tree standing opposite, some eight meters (!) above the ground. The artist climbed up the tree, attained the height of the rope, positioned himself properly on the rope and began, slowly and carefully putting one foot in front of the other, to cross the village square on the rope in the air (!). The tree limb on whose tip the rope was fastened was so overloaded by the weight of the artist that it broke, and the rope, with him, plummeted to the ground.

The artist had at that moment been in the air above the well and our master fell from the heavens in such a way that—no one would have thought it remotely possible—his back landed precisely on the crossbar of the well winch, his spinal column thus breaking exactly in the middle (!) so that his body, snapped in two, dangled over the well. The people were completely carried away, responded with enthusiastic applause, and burst into frenetic demonstrations of approval. General admiration, discussion, and comment were also elicited by the artist's quiet modesty and restrained manner. At last, once again, here was someone, who, by virtue of his noble character, his soul-stirring worldly wisdom, his exquisite and subtle humor, has no need to embrace those leftist, negativistic, modernistic tendencies which aid certain subversive elements, who, in the fateful and false guise of "art," would like nothing better than to undermine the natural order, the healthy discipline, and the simple sensitivity of our people; but they will not succeed, for we have seen once again that there are still people with b a c k-b o n e and character, who speak to the public from the depth of their souls, whose hearts are in the right place, who know their oats, and who know what's what. It is imperative that we make mention of the fact that the artist accomplished his program entirely from memory (!), by heart, and without the use of any notes whatsoever, a singular, colossal, and absolutely phenomenal feat of memory, which stands tall and unequaled.

One would hope that this performance will not remain the first and last of its kind, but such performances will take place more often, which would go far toward broadening the horizons of our school-age youngsters, enhancing their education, stimulating and supplementing their knowledge; while, at the same time, they would represent an extremely necessary factor in and vital contribution to the advancement of adult education. The performance was successfully concluded. Thanks are due the enterprising organizers without whose exemplary and flawless work this memorably choice artistic delight could not have been made possible!

A big round of applause.

The Village Square

The village square is empty.

You can see the street sweeper coming out from behind the town hall; he pulls a four-wheeled cart behind him; the side boards of the cargo space are painted yellow; the street sweeper carries a shovel and a broom on his back, he supports the handles laid across his shoulders with his right hand, with his left he pulls the cart.

You can see him sweep the leaves onto the shovel with the broom, lift the shovel filled with leaves, turn it over the opening of the cart's cargo space; you can see the foliage fall into the cart; he lowers the shovel again, pushes its sharpened iron front edge into a crack between stone slabs, sweeps more leaves with the broom; you can hear the broom's bristles swish across the stone.

He has swept one half of the square and begins to clear the other half, while on the half of the village square just cleared of leaves new leaves are again falling from the trees, are being precisely distributed over the surface by the wind; and while the street sweeper has been sweeping the leaves on the second half of the village square, the first half of the village square has again been covered by new leaves that have fallen from the trees in the meantime, have been precisely distributed over the surface by the wind. The street sweeper begins to sweep the first half of the village square again; I can hear his cursing, grumbling, and muttering

—*ya leaves fall here fall there 'n' fall 'n' i gotta sweep 'n' sweep 'n' sweep ya leaves ya trees ya.*

The stone, which becomes visible under the movements of the broom, glistens in the light that falls through the branches, while on the second half of the village square just cleared, leaves again begin to fall. The street sweeper's broom swishes in the cracks; the street sweeper wears short pants, holey shoes, rolled-down socks, has hairy legs, is naked from the waist up, his head bald, sweat glistens on his skin; he pulls the cart from one swept place to the next not-yet-swept place, dragging broom and shovel behind him, while the leaves fall and fall from the branches, I see new shoots growing from the scars in the branches, small green shoots, enlarging, enlarging into leaves, which then fall down again, while new shoots again sprout out of the branches and again . . .

. . . only the symbols, names, numbers, carved into the bark, heart, arrow . . .

. . . and the signs on the trunks with the inscription

STOPPING UNDER OLD TREES

STOPPING UNDER TREES

ESPECIALLY IN WIND AND STORMS IS DANGEROUS

THOSE WHO DO NOT COMPLY

MUST SUFFER THE CONSEQUENCES

SECTION 42, MUNICIPAL DEPARTMENT OF PARKS.

The Bridge

Before you reach the foothills, you have to cross the river.

Along the bank, life preservers are mounted on posts every five hundred meters. On the signs below the life preservers are the following instructions:

USE OF LIFE PRESERVERS

DO NOT REMOVE ROPE FROM SACK

HOLD ONTO ROPE NOOSE WITH ONE HAND

AND THROW LIFE PRESERVER IN FRONT OF SWIMMER

ROPE WILL SLIP OUT OF SACK

UNAUTHORIZED USE IS PUNISHABLE BY LAW.

You will reach the bridge.

The bridge can be entered only through doors on both sides.

On either side of the bridge five meters behind the bridgehead on the bridge itself is a door frame, one on each side of the river; in the door frames are wooden doors, the lower halves of the doors consisting of individual square wooden panels made of boards joined together without gaps; the upper halves of the doors are made of wooden slats, similar to louvered wooden doors or rabbit hutch openings;

the doors have padlocks; chains form ellipses around the outer right wooden slats and door-frame posts; they are secured with combination locks; the door handles are dull, the iron having turned gray from the murky air that keeps rising from the river, the handles squeak when they are pressed down; the beams, boards, and frames have been painted with a khaki and a grass green oil paint and varnished; the color glistens;

the glistening is interrupted by the moving shadows of the shrubs along the banks.

On both banks of the river little houses have been built there for the rotating bridgekeepers, in whose custody are the keys, in whose brains are the numbers which open the combination locks on the chains. If you want to cross the bridge, you must first go to the little bridgekeeper house, knock at the door of the little bridgekeeper house,

whereupon the window of the little bridgekeeper house will open;

the head of the bridgekeeper on duty will appear in it to see just who wants to go across the bridge;

the head will disappear inside of the window; afterwards the door of the little bridgekeeper house will open, the bridgekeeper on duty will appear in it in all his greatness and might;

he will give you a sign that you should come with him; together with you he will walk to the bridge, in his hands the jangling, dangling key; he will undo the ellipse of chain with the combination lock, ordering you to put your closed palms over your eyes so that you cannot see the number which opens the lock; he will unlock the door, opening the door to clear the way across the bridge for you; you will step onto the bridge; the bridgekeeper on duty, however, will again close the bridge door behind you, while you start on your way across the bridge to the other bank of the river; the bridgekeeper on duty will pull a lever above the door frame, whereupon you will hear the brief, clear ringing of a bell; I forgot to tell you earlier that above the door frames are bells whose clappers glisten because the river casts its reflection on them; the bell is rung so that the bridgekeeper on duty on the other bank of the river knows that someone is now coming across the bridge,

> under the bridge there are ships and small boats without cargo space without a hold for the passenger of the vehicle whoever travels in the boat down the river to the sea stands on the smooth boat surface which is facing away from the water feet spread so that the outer edges of the soles of the naked feet visible to the onlooker from both banks of the river are a half meter from the two outer boat surface edges which converge up front at a sharp angle rocking fifteen centimeters above the

water and visible to the onlooker from both banks of the river and in his fists he holds horizontally at chest height an extremely long wooden pole whose two ends touch the land the bank and with which you see him steadying the boat's movement on the waves on both sides to prevent a toppling of the boat to the left or right between its piers you see the skippers passing under the bridge standing upright on the beech larch alder aspen spruce willow cedar fir or oak wood while you stand above the planks the boats are smooth converging elongated surfaces fourteen meters long but six meters wide almost rectangles whose forward edges however have lost their true corners because the boat builder has sanded them down as required so that the two long sides continue and converge at a sharp angle after approximately four or more meters in the most widely varied congruent curved sections

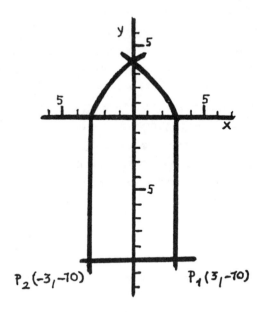

Fig. 2

without surface variations without a hold for the boat's passenger similar to common plywood sheets which nine- or ten- or eleven- or twelve-year-old boys cut out to make jumping jacks with moving legs painting them red green yellow white or indigo for the moldy papered walls in the smoky kitchen of september

and while the bridgekeeper on duty again disappears behind the door of his little bridgekeeper house, on the other bank of the river the window of the little bridgekeeper house on the other side opens; the head of the bridgekeeper on duty on the other bank will appear in it to see just who is coming across the bridge; the head will again disappear in the window, whereupon, a bit later, the door of the little bridgekeeper house on the other bank will open, the bridgekeeper will appear in it in all his greatness and might, come out, walk toward the bridge door on the other bank, which you keep approaching, will open it, receive you, who will by now have reached the end of the bridge and therefore the other bank of the river, will give you a nice friendly smile, while, on what now for you has long since become the other side of the river, the head of the aforementioned bridgekeeper will appear in the window of the little bridgekeeper house on what now for you has long since become the other side of the river, to see whether the bridgekeeper—for you this has been some time ago—indeed opens the bridge door for you here, enabling you to leave the bridge; he will wave at the bridgekeeper opening the door for you, calling out a friendly word such as
—*bridgewood bridgeiron*
and the like;
the bridgekeeper opening the door for you will for his part answer him with a friendly wave of the handkerchief and call
—*bridgeiron bridgewood*
and the like;
while you leave the bridge through the open door, the bridgekeeper on duty again closes the door, the clatter of the chain and the combination lock, the squeaking of the bridge door handles; the bridgekeeper on duty disappears into his little bridgekeeper house, while you go contentedly on your way;
both windows of the little bridgekeeper houses close, on the black panes

the river's reflection which rises up the embankment, while the two bridgekeepers on duty
turn the elliptical window latches of the little bridgekeeper houses from the vertical to the horizontal.
When the bell clappers are broken the two bridgekeepers on duty communicate simply by calling to each other loudly and clearly. They stand upright on the banks of the river with legs spread thirty degrees, raise their hands with elbows angled, and cup their hands, wrists and palms, and closed fingers to form a hollow, open cylinder around their wide-open lips, out of which their lonely calls reach over the river spanning the land or skimming the river's waves to the sea.

BRIDGEKEEPERS have the following RIGHTS AND DUTIES:

BRIDGE ORDINANCE
§ 1
1. The bridgekeeper can, that is to say, he has the duty to, turn away any individual appearing AT ALL SUSPICIOUS to him, he, the bridgekeeper, can and must deny him access to the bridge, prohibit the crossing of the river.
2. a) If the individual does not appear suspicious to the first bridgekeeper and he grants this individual access to the bridge, but to the second bridgekeeper on the other bank of the river the individual does appear AT ALL SUSPICIOUS, the latter on the other bank of the river has the right and duty to turn the individual back, to deny him exit from the bridge.
b) For the individual, who in such a case has no alternative but to go back over the bridge the way he just came, the first bridgekeeper, who earlier admitted him, the individual, must again open the gate so that the individual appearing at all suspicious only to the second bridgekeeper may leave the bridge again.
c) If it is indeed determined during the individual's progress across the bridge that the individual is a CRIMINAL, then it is the duty of both bridgekeepers to detain that particular individual on the bridge between the

two locked doors until the law enforcement authorities have been notified, the local police are able to appear at the scene to take, pick up, apprehend, and arrest the individual on the spot.

d) In times of such contingencies all other civilian bridge traffic is to be halted by the two bridgekeepers; without exception people must wait until the male or female criminal is safely in custody.

FOOTNOTE:

To be sure, experience has shown that for the most part criminals detained in this way jump from the bridge, where they are suddenly detained, into the river and swim away; usually, however, to avoid any such danger from the outset, they never take the way across the bridge, but ordinarily cross the river by various other means.

What is the result?

Only criminals who are too cowardly to jump into the river and, most of all, criminals who are nonswimmers could and can be apprehended and arrested on the bridge.

BRIDGE ORDINANCE

§ 2

The bridgekeepers may not demand any money for the crossing of the bridge, no toll is to be paid for the bridge crossing, in order to eliminate from the outset any possibility of bribery.

FOOTNOTE:

It is, nevertheless, left up to the individual to give the bridgekeepers on duty "gratuities" if so desired.

What is the result of all these regulations?

Any individual appearing at all suspicious to either one of the two bridgekeepers has no chance to cross the river officially.

FOOTNOTE:

To be sure, experience has shown that such people, compelled by this ongoing practice, have developed into the best swimmers in the land; some of them have already opened small swimming schools near the river, which enjoy great popularity among the people, and many parents send their children there from an early age.

What possibilities does the rejected individual still have for crossing the bridge?

Although bridgekeepers are generally considered incorruptible, the individual can, nevertheless, attempt to bribe the bridgekeepers on duty.

For the most part, however, this is n o t successful.

In such a case the individual goes to the nearest AUTHORITY IN CHARGE of such matters to obtain the so-called BRIDGE PHOTO IDENTITY CARD. Individuals who can prove their identity with a bridge photo identity card may not be turned away by the bridgekeeper unless the individual appears QUESTIONABLE to the bridgekeeper.

> BRIDGE ORDINANCE
>
> § 3
>
> QUESTIONABLE INDIVIDUALS, even though they possess a bridge photo identity card, can and must be turned away by the bridgekeeper because, among other things, IDENTITY CARD FORGERY may be, but does not have to be, a possibility or actuality.

FOOTNOTE:

There are times in which, on principle, all individuals appear suspicious or else questionable to the bridgekeepers. Individuals possessing bridge photo identity cards who appear questionable to the bridgekeeper and are therefore turned away by him, yet whose identity cards are in no way forged but are the REAL thing, may obtain a s e c o n d bridge photo identity card from the nearest authority in charge of such matters.

> BRIDGE ORDINANCE
>
> § 4
>
> Individuals with two valid bridge photo identity cards can be turned away by the bridgekeeper only in unforeseen EXCEPTIONAL CASES.

THE BRIDGE PHOTO IDENTITY CARD:

Without exception there is a one-year waiting period for the SCRUTINY of the

IMPECCABLE CIVIC INTEGRITY

as well as

POLITICAL HYGIENE AND CLEANLINESS of the individual

provided for in the public health regulations.

FEES:

The sum total of today's date in local currency,

plus unspecified sums for stamp duties.

What is the purpose of all this?

Suspicious or questionable individuals, as the case may be, will n o t have the opportunity
to concentrate,
gather,
assemble,
amass,
band together,
hold meetings,
take up collections,
in one part of the country
but will be evenly distributed on both sides of the river.

BRIDGE ORDINANCE

§ 5

With regard to possible errors or harm, as long as these do not concern civil matters, bridgekeepers can neither be held accountable nor be prosecuted because the general view is that TO ERR IS HUMAN.

BRIBING OF OFFICIALS

for the purpose of reducing the waiting period for the bridge photo identity card is n o t possible, but is usually done. It helps to bring the officials potted flowers, azaleas perhaps, no cut flowers, or else a cask of recently distilled fruit brandy. Supposedly this is not at all frowned upon, some say this sort of thing is even encouraged by higher authorities. It is supposedly hoped that this will bring the officials closer to the people. The officials make themselves popular by accepting same and by helping the people in return.

That is a known fact.

There are even a lot of people who say this particular kind of bureaucracy was introduced f o r t h e s o l e p u r p o s e of giving the officials an opportunity to get to know the people better, to become more involved with the people, as well as, on the other hand, to enable the people to get to know the officials, to become somewhat more involved with them, the officials:

a PURELY PEDAGOGICAL measure for a better general UNDERSTANDING of each other.

Therefore, in higher circles, that official is considered the most capable and best who has the most potted flowers at home and who gets drunk the most often on fruit brandy.

Yes, sir.

You remember, while you go on toward the bridge, the moving shadows of the shrubs near the doors, the gray board rails and planks on top of the bridge metal, the gray door handles which have taken on the color of the river from the air which continually touches the waves of the river and rises.

the ancient drainage system still in operation today only the pipes replaced otherwise always been in perfect shape you can make out the patterns of the underground systems by the one-half-meter-wide sod and determine the direction of the invisibly flowing water

and

a couple of things i forgot to mention though

the empty concrete forms on the banks of the streams too but above all on the edge of the river the water mains and the paper between the shrubs left behind in back of the empty concrete forms where on sundays they put up umbrellas and picnic spread brown blankets on the sandy ground put bread on the cloth skewer beef but on weekdays

and

what remains to be mentioned among other things

the geometrically surveyed points in the landscape these are one-meter-tall cylinders r = 1.5 m stones held together by mortar sometimes storks or cranes nest on them the round surveyed points in the landscape visible from far away and clearly evident in the following pattern

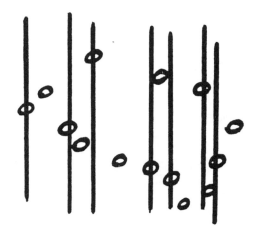

Fig. 3

no point in its straight extension intersects a second point and always
no matter where you go you come upon some kind of triangulation
point made of stone whereby you can readily calculate your location

The Village Square

—*The village square is empty.*
—*We can walk across the village square.*
In the center the well.
Between the stones moss is growing. When it buds you can see white dots in the green tufts, separated from one another by tenth-of-a-millimeter-thin lines of black soil.
Before the front doors you can see ascending and descending stairs leading upward and downward into the houses.
On the wooden doors you can see the rings which are grasped and struck against the doors by the hands of the exchanging visitors. The metal is worn, it smells like wet brass; you can hear the metal rings knocking on the wood.
The doors open.
The figures disappear into the black corridors behind them, into the stairwells, anterooms, vestibules; you can hea 'heir steps fading in the interior of the buildings while the doors have long since been closed again.

> yes that's right outside the village grain is being threshed the wagons pulled by black cattle are five-axled each axle ten wheels they roll over the grain yellow between the wheels grains are separated from stalks the grains arranged in a circle the stalks arranged in a circle alongside with their sticks herders flail the black coats of the cattle dust rises from the welts left by the sticks

You can see the doors open. The visitors step out again, turn back toward the black door openings, raise their right hands, while the doors have long since been shut again.

—*Let's walk across the village square.*
—*The village square is empty.*

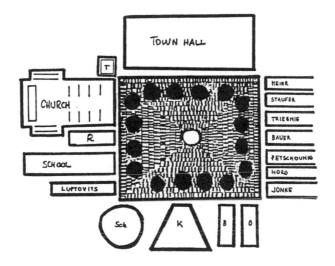

T = Tower
R = Rectory
Sch = Scheliessnig (Blacksmith)
K = Kullnig (General Store)
B = Bierbaumer
O = Obernosterer

(—... the experience of the conflict between the world of objects and the world of people in which the world of objects dictates patterns to the world of people...

—... the village square is a structural model...)

Fig. 4 The Village Square

41

No, that's a lie, because there are t r e e   s t u m p s along the edges of the square, the round, smooth surfaces of wood, the remains of cutoff trunks, circular, neat circles, each with a diameter of approximately one and a half meters.

The teacher has come out of the school building with the children and has shown them the circles of wood.

Much earlier, though, the teacher had also put away his chalk after finishing the drawing on the board, the diagram of the village square with the well in the center. Along the edges he had written into each of the rectangles representing the houses the names of the owners of the houses gathered around the square:

Meier, Staufer, Triebnig, Bauer, Petschounig, Moro, Jonke, Kullnig, Luptovits, Scheliessnig, Bierbaumer, Obernosterer.

He had drawn the stones on the ground into the area representing the village square;

—*the village square is paved with 1,946 white stone slabs.*

On the other half of the board he had drawn a side view of the well, in order to explain to the children the function of the well winch.

—*The well winch holds the rope, which is rolled up. If you crank to the right the rope is pulled up so that the water-filled bucket comes up from the depth of the earth's interior; but if you crank to the left or if you let go of the winch, the rope is unwound again so that the bucket crashes beneath the skin of the planet to draw fresh water from its unknown depth.*

With his hands gesticulating through the air in the classroom, he told them to imitate the various appropriate well-winch-turning movements, shortly after which, all the hands of the children that were present closed to fists as if many invisible graspable well-winch-turning handles were floating through the classroom atmosphere.

The teacher had drawn on the left side of the board next to the village square diagram a side view of the town hall building, also of the school building, on the right next to the picture of the well, the church with its spire and the rectory, in the rectory the open rectory office window, in it the head of the priest peeking out the window, next to the priest's head he had drawn his right hand with the index finger raised, on the left half of the board he had the mayor step out of the door of the town hall side view, had slipped a file under his right arm, and explained to the children his position of leadership in the village.

—*The mayor is the top man in the village; everything he does is for the good of the village; if he weren't there to enforce the prevailing law of the land, the village would disintegrate in no time; and he always has to write a lot, but, for that, he has an efficient female secretary or a competent male secretary, who makes work a little easier for him.*

The teacher had told the children to stop whenever they see the mayor and to do so as soon as he appears far off on the horizon to be coming toward them, take off their hats or caps, greet him properly, and, in doing so, have only to nod their heads; as he had strongly recommended that they show respect to their elders in general, especially parents, grandparents, aunts, uncles, great aunts, great uncles, and all other close and distant or distant close relatives, for the latter are their role models, keep in mind the experiences that they have handed down, and act exactly according to and not differently from them, because with them in mind one might spare himself and his own life a lot that they had already been through for us and overcome.

—Furthermore:

Children should not play with matches, knives, forks, and scissors, that's for sure,

but later, too, if one is to fare well, one should honor them by shining his shoes and brushing his teeth at least twice each day,

one thoroughly washes himself in the evening, of course, and one does not do things halfway,

one thinks democratically,

one always keeps a clean handkerchief in his pants pocket,

one does not abuse social institutions,

one does today what will be good for all of us tomorrow, because in a few years he will still have time for everything else,

whenever one meets someone, one greets him in a friendly manner, especially if one can't stand that person,

one fulfills his civic duties,

one does not ask impertinent questions,

one follows the instructions of the conductor on public conveyances,

43

one does not read obscene books, novels, and the like,
one does not lean out the window in the middle of a trip
  but rather,
one closes the windows and doors in the winter so that the toilet doesn't
  freeze up,
one does not pester women,
one steps down facing forward, the left hand without fail on the left front
  and not the rear handrail,
one does not come late,
one does not put off until the day after tomorrow what he can do today,
but why not try to get some of it done by noon tomorrow,
one does not use the toilets during stops in train stations,
one does not come late,
one checks the safety catch of his firearm on a regular basis to see that it is
  always in the correct position,
one does not hang around shady establishments,
one does not run away if he hears or feels himself being called, but stops
  immediately in order to comply as soon as possible with imminent ex-
  pectations,
one submits as fully as possible to the powers that be,
one blows his nose into his handkerchief and does not draw the mucous
  up his nose, also, one does not smear the contents removed while pick-
  ing his nose onto his host's curtains,
one does not offer resistance to the authority of the state,
  but, rather,
one pulls up his pant legs before sitting down so that the crease stays in,
when eating, one usually takes the fork in his left hand, the knife in his
  right,
one does not simply piss into the washbasin in his hotel room but goes out
  into the hall and looks for the proper facilities that have been expressly
  made available for such purposes,
one votes for the party to which he belongs,
whenever one coughs or yawns, he should be so kind as to cover his mouth
  with his hand;
and finally:

one does not slouch, does not carouse, does not kill, does not annoy, does not change, does not screw, does not make any noise, does not beat, does not love, does not gorge, does not booze, does not defy, does not lie, does not steal, does not gossip, does not shout, does not brag,
but, rather,
one leads, prays, brushes, confesses, straightens, suffers, rides, rides, rides (through day and night to the end of the continent at the beginning of the ocean, where one will sell his horse at the shore in order to have at his disposal money for renting a seaworthy rowboat),
further:
one does, combs, learns, honors, sees, greets, goes, seeks, hurries, looks, runs, helps, races, strains, fights, lends, sifts, lets, eats, blows his nose, tracks, rubs, flashes, nourishes, dashes, gives, is useful, consumes, hangs, cleans, washes, dyes, bleaches, darns, sews, knits, files, embroiders, aims, follows, wherever he can.
Coming back to the church and the rectory, the teacher had explained to the children the function of the priest drawn with index finger raised looking out the illustrated window of the illustrated rectory next to the illustrated well on the right side of the board; in doing so, he had pointed to the illustrated church next to the sketched rectory with the pointer which he had taken from the left corner of the room next to the board.
—One goes to church every Sunday without exception,
one does not make fun of the priest's habit, even though when he's wearing it he may look like a scarecrow, because it is a symbol of his high office,
one does not blaspheme God, much less does one anger Him, nor those who are closer to Him than we,
one does not come late to services on Sunday or on weekdays, nor does one miss them through his own fault or negligence, nor does one keep others from them,
in church one is not immodest in dress and not too free with members of the opposite sex,
but behaves solemnly,
one opens and closes the door quietly, even if the hinges haven't been recently oiled,
one walks on tiptoe,

one dips his right index finger into the water-filled holy water font next to the door inside and not beforehand into the rain barrel outside in front of the gate,

one touches his forehead with the finger moistened as previously described, and not with the dry one, moving once from top to bottom and once from left to right,

one does not think anything indecent, unpleasant, unclean, immodest, impure, unchaste, nor does one lust for such things in church or anywhere else,

one does not make a racket,

one listens to the words of the preaching priest and remembers them, even though something might seem to him to be rather dumb because he is not yet smart enough to be able to understand it,

one does not sin in church through curious or rude, lustful looks,

one does not laugh, nor does one giggle,

one does not touch himself or others indecently in church, even if one is well acquainted with them,

one lets the stillness and the silence affect himself,

one reflects upon himself,

however, shortly before, one should go to the toilet, so that later on he won't have to hold it back for hours.

The teacher had drawn for the children on the left half of the board, next to the illustrated church, a cross section of the holy water font, symbolizing the water in the calotte-shaped hollow of the basin in the form of wavy lines, next to it the altar, the wood-carved choir railings in front of the altar, the pulpit, the row of pews. He told the children that these were said to be very valuable, old, and truly beautiful wood carvings. He explained the shapes of the ornamentation carved into the wood, all kinds of wood-carved ornamentation found in the church, circles, squares, ellipses, semicircles, rectangles, semiellipses, sectors of circles, triangles, segments of ellipses. He had drawn into the shapes and their derivatives representing the carved ornamentation, center points and center lines, in the circles and ellipses inserted points and lines so that faces with eyebrows, foreheads, hairlines, eyes, noses, nostrils, and lips were formed.

—Such shapes and faces were carved into the pews, into the altar, into the

choir railings, and into the pulpit many years ago by a great and distinguished wood carving artist, or sculptor, as one can also call someone like that; this man must have been a great master, he took a sharp knife and with it cut into the wood the shapes that I drew on the board for you, a difficult and artistic task; the wood chips lay on the church floor; and then the sexton came along with a broom and dustpan and swept up the wood chips lying on the floor.

In those days, many, many years ago, the artist is said to have come into the village one day before he began with his work and to have been invited by the priest of that time for some hot beef soup; the priest of that time reports on this in the village chronicle:

In the evening he came into the village; I took him in. He spent the night in the guest room; in the morning we sat together at breakfast; there was white bread and coffee; then all of a sudden he leaned over to me and whispered in my ear

—I'm a distinguished wood-carver but please don't tell anyone, because I am running away, am being pursued by my enemies, my adversaries, I had outcarved them, and that went against their grain, and they are still out to kill me, but up to now I've eluded them, secretly harbored by the shadowy chambers at the edges of the forest, then stole away into the most wretched parts of the moor and the marshes, for days hidden in a cave, until I was sure that they had given up their search for the time being; then I took the road across the mountains, nourished myself with dried roots, chewed on toadstools, now and then I brewed herbal tea, until finally I came here to you.

—Couldn't you speak a bit louder; I don't hear well, am almost deaf.

—But if someone should be eavesdropping?

—There is no one here.

—In the wilderness I warmed my hands over the fire, its smoke rising into my eyes until tears flowed out of them like torrents of light rushing into the forest through the branches and forcing my face to the ground, buried in the odor of decayed leaves and needles; I sat there, my hands clasped behind my head, and lamented my fate as king of the wood-carvers threat-

47

*ened by his enemies and adversaries, for whom, in good faith and in an
effort to delight and amaze them, I carved from all the tree trunks in their
orchards lifelike saint statues looking as if they had grown right from the
ground, whose thick heads of hair bore abundant fruit; but please tell this
to no one, and I only told you about it because you are a priest and can be
trusted.*

—God loves the persecuted.
—But for me He has no pity.
—Especially for you, don't you see it?
—I am still running away.
*—A sign for you: There is work; an entire church is at your disposal, pews,
choir railings, a pulpit, and an altar; free room and board.*
—But what if someone should see me?
*—You are under my protection, under the protection of the Church, under
the protection of the village.*
*Then the man took a sharp knife out of his pouch, and I went with him at
once into the church; he worked all of fourteen days, every day from
morning till night, with the knife carving indentations, grooves, figures,
and faces into the wood; the shavings and wood chips lay on the church
floor; then the sexton came along with dustpan and broom and swept up
the wood chips.*

The teacher explained to the children that the priest had recorded this story
in the village chronicle; that's why we know about it.
*—The old village chronicle is a large, thick, and heavy book; its pages have
turned yellow in all those years; it has been filled for a long time and is
preserved as a valuable treasure in the rectory library. If you ask Father
nicely for it, he'll show it to you. To this day he still enters everything that
happens into a book, into a new one, but one which will also be filled very
soon; such things are called "sources for historiography."*
The teacher had drawn the village chronicle for the children near the
middle of the lower edge of the board under the diagram of the village
square. Then he had put away the chalk, had the children line up two by two
in front of the classroom door, opened a cabinet in the corridor, took out a

large school compass, and led the children through the corridor and the open school door out to the village square; he had ordered them to line up in a row.

There are tree stumps along the edges of the square, round, with a diameter of one and a half meters, the cut surfaces of wood, the remains of cutoff trunks, the cut surfaces glisten in the sun.

He has come out of the school building with the children and shown them the circles of wood.

He takes the large school compass, places its point into the center of the tree stump, lets the end of the other compass branch, which is suspended freely in the air, touch the circumference of the circle-shaped tree stump, traces the circle with the compass, following the circumference of the tree stump.

—*This is a circle, the surface of this tree stump is a circle.*

He removes the compass from the tree stump, leaning it against the wall of the house in back of him.

The children sit down on the tree stumps.

The House of the Blacksmith

The house of the blacksmith is of white limestone; the house of the black-smith is round; the layout of the house of the blacksmith is a circle with a radius of seven meters.

The house was designed years ago by the village architect of that time and was built

by the old blacksmith,

his wife

and his son, the present blacksmith.

They baked the bricks themselves; at that time, years ago,

the old blacksmith,

his wife

and his son, the present blacksmith,

were heard working till late into the night; the stones clattered, the fire cast its shadows everywhere. Over the fire they baked the bricks. They baked the bricks themselves. But they only used the bricks for the foundation of the house; then, it seems, they felt that the brick-baking was, in a word, too foolish, too much trouble; for the next level they stacked on top of each other squared blocks of ordinary limestone from the mountains.

They mixed their own mortar, with a wooden pole. In this way, years ago, the old blacksmith,

his wife

and his son, the present blacksmith,

took turns standing in front of a wood-framed rectangle, they had jammed four one-meter and four half-meter-long, twenty-centimeter-wide boards into the ground in front of what was then the building site in such a way that all at once two sandboxlike containers were formed, in which they took turns mixing their own mortar with a two-meter-long pole; with the pole they are said to have stirred the mortar;

the old blacksmith,

his wife

and his son, the present blacksmith,

took turns

dipping the pole into the wet mortar, going back and forth with the pole in the wobbly mortar mass, and the movement of the pole caused surface variations in the thick gray liquid, a line in the gray in the shape of a groove from the base of which the wet mortar moved up five millimeters along the sides, but the mortar surface immediately smoothed out again, whenever

the old blacksmith

or his wife

or his son, the present blacksmith,

stopped shoving the pole through the thick, wet gray. The gray groove is said to have trailed for a half meter behind the pole, behind the half-meter zone behind the pole in the mortar the groove supposedly became level again, rising up to even out the sticky mortar mass lying horizontal in the sandbox.

At that time, years ago, all the children of the village are said to have always gathered around the sandbox to gaze at the moving mortar. They say not a single child laughed. All are said to have been spellbound by what for them was the demonic movement of the mortar in the sandbox. It is unbelievable, they say, that children could all of a sudden be so quiet. That was due solely to the mortar, say the people in the village. Then, one day, a few children are said to have plucked the grass that had been growing along the bottoms of the side walls of the sandboxes. Because of the plucking of the grass that had been growing along the sides of the wooden walls of the sandboxes, the boards are said to have become loose every once in a while; and because the grass tufts, while they were growing, had dug their roots under the boards, gaps are supposed to have formed in the sandbox, and every once in a while, say the people in the village, a little of the mortar mixture leaked out of the sandbox through the gaps. The old blacksmith, they say, saw that and chased away the children who had gathered around the sandbox to watch the wet mortar by scolding them in his surly way. The children ran away and suddenly began to laugh and scream again. At home then they all got a beating because their parents had heard that they had bothered the old blacksmith while he was building his house by plucking the grass tufts which had been growing out along the sides of the sandboxes, and that's why the mortar had leaked out every once in a while. The parents are said to have really gotten after their children then and screamed

—just wait I'm gonna give it to ya botherin' the old blacksmith when he's buildin' his house pullin' out grass so that all th' mortar leaks out.

Throughout the village, one is then said to have heard for a good half hour the shrieking and bawling of the children who got a beating from their parents because they plucked the grass along the sides of the sandboxes on the building site of the old blacksmith. From the open windows of the houses one heard the slaps ringing on the faces of the children, this is said to have resulted in a real smacking of parents' skin on children's skin. On top of it some parents are said to have pulled down their children's pants and worked their naked behinds over, beating them with their hard, calloused palms. The parents, say the people in the village, had let their palms fall from one half to three quarters of a meter onto the children's paling naked behinds, approximately one half second later moved back to the same height again, and repeated this movement twenty to fifty times until the skin of the children's quivering buttocks was completely reddened by the spanks.

In the village they favor a strict upbringing. Better their pants down too often than never at all, is the opinion generally held in the village. Better once too much than never enough. The old blacksmith, as he heard the children's screams that time, is supposed to have smiled benevolently and said

—the more often the pants are down, the better; the more often you pull a child's pants down, the easier he'll learn to bear his hard lot later on.

Whenever the mortar in the sandbox was mixed enough, say the people in the village,

either the old blacksmith

or his wife

or his son, the present blacksmith,

took an old washbasin, white and having black cracks (due to chipped enamel), stuck it into the mixed mortar until the mixed mortar flowed into the washbasin, took the filled washbasin out of the sandbox, carried it to the started wall, where, then,

either the old blacksmith

or his wife

or his son, the present blacksmith,

spread the wet mortar from the washbasin onto the surface of the stacked blocks with a trowel and laid another row of blocks or bricks.

As the house had gotten taller,

the old blacksmith

and his wife

and his son, the present blacksmith,

then built a wooden scaffolding, on which, then,

either the old blacksmith

or his wife

or his son, the present blacksmith,

stood, is said to have had the white, black-speckled washbasin handed up to him, and up there spread the wet mortar with a trowel onto the stacked blocks and laid another row of blocks.

Later,

the old blacksmith

or his wife

or his son, the present blacksmith,

is then said to have come upon the idea that one could actually use a kind of block-and-tackle-like hoist,

and

either the old blacksmith

or his wife

or perhaps his son, the present blacksmith,

is said to have gone to the sawmill owner and asked him if he had a round wooden disk, a wooden wheel, two centimeters thick and with a diameter of one decimeter, whereupon the sawmill owner is said to have walked around in a circle in his sawmill three times and then finally pulled out from the wood waste, from a pile of wood scraps and shavings, a wooden wheel one and a half centimeters thick and with a diameter of twelve centimeters. The people in the village say the sawmill owner supposedly said that the wooden disk came from the top of a twenty-meter-high spruce that he'd had chopped down on the north slope, costing a woodcutter his life, granted just a foreign worker, thank God; the heavy spruce is supposed to have fallen with its whole weight on top of the worker, too late in getting out of the way; afterwards, he, the sawmill owner, had the spruce stripped, the trunk cut into boards, the boards sold to the carpenter; the carpenter built window cases for the innkeeper out of them; and to this day, the sawmill owner reportedly said, according to the people in the village, one can admire the wood in the windows of the inn; and from the top of this spruce, the sawmill owner reportedly said, according to the people in the village, also comes the little wooden wheel which he, the sawmill owner, happened to find in the waste among the wood shavings and chips, and he, the sawmill owner, according to the people in the village, put the wooden wheel into the hand of

either the old blacksmith

or his wife

or his son, the present blacksmith,

when asked about the price, said

—*that doesn't cost anything, that's ridiculous, merely an act of friendship and in keeping with the spirit of the village,*

whereupon

either the old blacksmith

or his wife

or his son, the present blacksmith,

thanked the sawmill owner very kindly and carried the wooden wheel to the building site where, then,

either the old blacksmith

or his son

took a knife, carved a groove into the outer edge of the wheel, drilled a hole into the center of the wheel, after that speared the wheel on a pole of the wooden scaffolding lying at a right angle to the wall of the started house, and fitted a rope into the carved groove of the wooden wheel, whereupon the old blacksmith

or his wife

or his son, the present blacksmith,

fastened the white, black-speckled washbasin onto the lower end of the rope with a noose and hoisted it by means of the block-and-tackle-like contraption.

At that time, years ago, one could hear till late into the night the sound of mortar being mixed; the people in the village say one heard till very late into the night the thumping of the two-meter-long wooden pole which, in the course of the mixing movements in the sticky mortar, struck the edges of the boards in the sandbox, the slipping of the hemp rope in the guide of the wooden reel, the dipping of the washbasin's iron into the mortar (a piece of tin falling in slow motion, dipping into the water), the thumping of the washbasin's iron against the wood of the scaffolding, the hushed commands of the old blacksmith in the darkness, the steps in the sand whenever the washbasin was carried from the sandbox to the started wall to the scaffolding, or from the scaffolding from the started wall back to the sandbox, and the soft swishing of the hemp on the enamel and on the black chipped parts of the enamel.

For a short time, in those days, years ago,

the old blacksmith,

his wife

and his son, the present blacksmith,

supposedly had difficulties attaching the filled washbasin to the rope, say the people. The people in the village say the washbasin kept coming loose from the carefully tied noose, is said to have fallen down several times; and on the ground in front of the building site the mortar often flowed out of the fallen washbasin and spread over the ground. After that,

either the old blacksmith

or his wife

or his son, the present blacksmith,

is said to have been given by the storekeeper an old basket with a handle, into which they then put the washbasin filled with new mortar, fastened the lower end of the rope onto the basket handle, and then they hoisted the basket along with the washbasin up to the scaffolding. After that, they are said to have lost no more mortar, according to the people in the village.

But the village architect is also said to have been very helpful to the three of them while the house was being built in those days, years ago. Because the house of the blacksmith is round and a round house is not easy to build, the village architect is said to have gone once each day to the building site to say to the old blacksmith

—you have to put one block on top of the other in such a way that the bottom surface of the block lying above covers two upper-half surfaces of the two blocks lying underneath.

Before

the old blacksmith

with his wife

and with his son, the present blacksmith,

began building then, the village architect is said to have drawn a white circle for them on the desired place on the ground where the house was supposed to stand, later really did stand, and to this day still stands. Shortly before the start of the construction, the village architect is said to have spread on the hard, brown ground on which dried cow dung lay, a white powder which is said to be used in the city for marking the bounds as well as the center and sixteen-meter lines on athletic fields where soccer and team handball are played, and in such a manner he drew on the ground a white circle with a radius of seven meters for the layout of the future house. Along the outline of the circle

the old blacksmith,

his wife

and his son, the present blacksmith,

then built the exterior walls. And once each day, say the people in the village, the village architect would turn up at the building site, and one would hear the village architect remind the blacksmith of the fact

—you have to put one block on top of the other in such a way that the bottom surface of the block lying above covers two upper-half surfaces of the two blocks lying underneath.

In those days, years ago, they say, one could hear till late into the night the sound of mortar being mixed, the sound of wet mortar being spread on dry blocks and bricks, the spurting of small, wet lime globs out of the seams, and the tapping of one block on the other. Throughout the village and even far outside the village. Travelers who came into the village by night in those days are said to have heard the sounds of the building site and seen the fire of the building site from quite far off. The travelers said they thought wooden crates were being buried by torchlight down here in the village. Not until in the village itself then, the travelers are supposed to have said, would one see on the scaffolding of the building site

the body of the old blacksmith

or that of his wife

or that of his son, the present blacksmith,

standing out against the bright night sky. The travelers are supposed to have said one saw the body of whoever was working hanging on the scaffolding like a spider in the sky. And not until the last drunks left the inn is

the old blacksmith

said to have given

his wife

and his son, the present blacksmith,

the order to quit work;

the old blacksmith

or his wife

or his son, the present blacksmith,

whoever was just then between the wooden beams of the scaffolding spreading the mortar, is said to have stepped down from the scaffolding; whoever was mixing the mortar in the sandbox put the pole aside; the basin was washed out, the splashing of the water on the iron, the singing of the liquid swirling in the curves of the enamel, the hissing of the water poured onto the sand. Amidst the clamoring of the drunks who were being shown out the door by the innkeeper,

the old blacksmith,

his wife

and his son, the present blacksmith,

at that time, years ago,

ended the day's work and began the night's rest!

After seven months the house of the blacksmith is then said to have been

finished.
After the completion of the house
the old blacksmith
died,
his wife
followed him shortly thereafter,
and the son, the present blacksmith,
took over the house and the workshop.

Three meters above the ground the blacksmith built a roof over his work-shop. Under the roof the blacksmith has his tools. The roof, ring-shaped, protects the area around the house from rain, hail, and snow. The roof is three meters wide, it's made of tin, which is said to have darkened over the years under the influence of the weather. At one time the tin is said to have glistened in the sun. The people in the village say they couldn't look at the house of the blacksmith at noon because the tin always blinded them. In those days, the people are supposed to have said, the tin is so blinding that under the roof the blacksmith can't be seen at all. Under the blacksmith's roof it is night most of the time, the people in those days are said to have claimed. One could see only the fire next to the anvil, and the tongs that are held in the fire by the blacksmith's hand, and the horseshoe which, clamped between the pincers of the tongs, glows over the fire. But even now that one is no longer blinded by the roof's reflection because the tin mirror has grown dull in hailstorms, of course, it is no longer night under the blacksmith's roof, but it is continual twilight. The people in the village say the clouds of gloomy days had settled on the roof, giving and transfer-ring their cloudiness to the roof. The fire under the roof is transparent, and on some days it is more transparent than the air, brighter and more glisten-ing than the sun. When you look into the smithy's work space under the roof, look into the fire,

> you can see in the fire the storekeeper's house, which stands next to
> the round house of the blacksmith; the house of the storekeeper has
> the shape of an irregular truncated pyramid; the layout of the store-
> keeper's house is a trapezoid; in the fire you can see the windows of
> the storekeeper's house opening and on the second floor see the

storekeeper's wife and on the ground floor the storekeeper's daughter shaking the past night out of the sheets, feather beds, and blankets, into the morning;

so transparent and bright is the fire.

Next to the fire you can see the dark silhouette of the body of the blacksmith, whose hands reach for the tongs. His face is invisible

like that of the charcoal burner who stands in front of the

kiln and is enveloped by the smoke.

In front of the roof stand the shadows of the horses that are being shod. The horses themselves are u n d e r the roof, and in front of the roof, next to the house, you can see their shadows. Their hides glisten in the fire. The fire casts the shadows from their bodies out of the workshop into the day. The horses are led to the blacksmith's house through the exceedingly transparent morning air. You can see their bodies approaching in a trot through the white morning. Then they disappear under the roof into the twilight of the smithy.

The tin roof is supported by oiled wooden rafters. In the joints of the rafters live moths. At twilight their wings begin to flap out of the wood. Their chitins graze the rafters. In the morning you can now and then find one knocked dead at the wall, in the tin.

The Village Square

There are tree stumps along the edges of the square.

The children are sitting on the tree stumps. Three children per tree stump, their knees pressed closely together, their eyes turned toward the teacher, who is standing in front of the facade.

There must have been trees standing here at one time!

Yes, that's right, a short time ago there were still trees standing here, that's right, with symbols, names, numbers, carved into the bark, rectangle, fifteen, Joseph, sine, twenty-three, arc, eight, two, forty-six, G, F, Jonke, heart, Josephine, arrow . . . , and signs on the trunks,

DANGER DURING STORMY CONDITIONS STAND UNDER TREES AT YOUR OWN RISK. The trees shed their leaves, which the street sweeper swept up and threw into the cart.

Then all of a sudden the trees were chopped down because the branches had begun to grow into the roofs.

The branches had begun to bore into the roofs, had pushed through the tiles, had penetrated into the rafters.

You heard the boring of the branches pushing the tiles aside. You could have seen several tiles that had been touched by the leaves falling down, you could have heard several tiles striking the pavement of the village square and shattering. The creaking of the rafter beams being dislodged by the branches. The hissing and rumbling of junk being pushed aside in the attics.

It couldn't have gone on this way. The roofs would have shattered. Would have been pushed off the houses by the spreading treetops.

The tree next to the church smashed a spire window. The branch grew into the belfry. The twigs and leaves touched the bell. The tree was stirred by the wind, the branch struck and rang the bell in the church spire.

The trees would have pushed down the dusty mattresses, bedframes, brooms, shovels, commodes, ovens, kitchen stoves, credenzas, buckets, washstands, and spinning wheels stored in the attics; the junk, along with the attics, roofs, rafters, beams, tiles, and shingles, would have fallen behind the houses. The roofs and the junk would have lain behind the roofless houses; the people would have had to build new roofs, buy new beams and tiles, they would have had to pick up the junk behind the houses and carry it up to the attics again.

The growth of the trees had flourished to the point that several roofs were already seriously threatened.

The branches already were sticking in between the tiles, and inside the roofs the leaves already were touching, assaulting, attacking, and threatening the beam structures.

It couldn't have gone on this way.

That's why the woodcutters were called from the forests.

The woodcutters came from the forests.

They propped up the trees, yes, around the trees they wedged heavy beams, at angles, against the trunks, driving the supports into the ground of the village square.

Then they took axes, climbed the trees, and chopped off the branches.

The branches fell from the treetops. The branches fell from the trunks.

They cleared away the branches.

Then they took saws and sawed down the branchless trunks.

The trees fell slowly, haltingly, the supports preventing a quick tumbling down.

Branches and trunks were carried away.

Piled up at the edge of the village.

Supposed to be used for building lumber, firewood, or bridge timber.

Then the woodcutters returned to their forests again.

Disappeared in the shadows along the edges of the forests. For the last time, the street sweeper swept, cleared the village square, pushed wood chips, leftover twigs and leaves onto the shovel.

When he had swept the first half of the village square, he began to sweep the second half of the village square.

While he was sweeping the second half of the village square, no more leaves fell on the first half of the village square just swept, because there were no more trees there to shed leaves.

Then he also swept the second half of the village square.

You heard the swishing of the broom on the stone.

Then he disappeared behind the town hall, broom and shovel on his shoulders, pulling the cart behind him. The wood of the cargo space on the cart is painted yellow.

Then he left the village.

He wasn't needed anymore because there were no more leaves there to be swept.

He pulled the cart behind him and walked east toward the edge of the horizon.

I heard his cursing and grumbling.

—*No more leaves nothin' to sweep nothin' to sweep no more leaves no work no leaves.*

The wheels were heard skidding on the stones along the road for quite some time.

The street sweeper had lived in a shack behind the town hall. The shack stands empty; I see the open door, the empty room, the bare, brown walls.

There are tree stumps along the edges of the village square, circular.

It has been quite some time since the teacher disappeared with the children into the school building.

The wood's cut surfaces glisten in the sun.

People sit down on the stumps, perhaps it's afternoon, warm themselves in the air, and look at each other, look at passersby, and the passersby look at those sitting on the stumps.

Visits being exchanged.

Sleeping Positions

Some houses have flat roofs.

On hot nights it is common practice to sleep on the roofs.

The bedframes are carried up to the roofs over the stairs on the outside walls of the houses or over the stairways in the interior of the houses. Sheets, blankets, and feather beds too.

There are people who, from the outset, leave their beds on the roofs

during ing summer periods of atmospheric high pressure.

At night you can see figures disappear behind roof ledges, iron bedframes, and blankets.

In the morning the sheets gleam.

The figures rise, sit awhile in their beds among the wrinkles of the crumpled bed linens, stretch their arms, and yawn loudly.

Some have caps on their heads and read for another half hour. Then you can see the figures stand upright on the mattresses atop the bedsprings, and the iron coils squeak. They leave their beds, hop onto the roof surfaces, do their morning exercises by thrusting their bodies, their hands in particular, into the air and back again, and leave the roofs by way of the stairs outside or inside the walls.

In the morning the beds are usually carried down from the roofs, the iron frames grazing the walls; during continuous periods of atmospheric high pressure, however, it is common practice to leave the beds on the roofs. Then all day long you can see the iron bedframes on the roofs glistening in the sun.

In any case, however, the beds are made in the morning, whether in the houses or on the roofs.

Especially at noon, however, it is the custom of most people to wrap their heads in the latest newspaper purchased in the morning, to lie down in a narrow street or in the village square, and to sleep for a few hours.

The Village Square

—The village square is empty.
—We can walk across the village square.
—Let's walk across the village square.
—People are sitting in the café.

The café is built into a recess in the rock. As the extension of the stone ceiling—a rock ledge—a straw roof supported by posts.

Under the rock roof to the left, the kettle, the stove, and straight ahead, benches, chairs, and tables, all painted green.

Behind them, on the interior rock wall, three reliefs hewn out of the rock depicting the café owner, who is, first, standing in front of the stove and brewing coffee, second, just turning away from the stove and turning toward a customer sitting on a bench to bring him coffee, and, third, standing in front of the customer sitting on the bench and serving up the coffee.

In the rock floor under the straw roof, a basin, through which flows the stream from the mountains; its current is calmed by a sluice that was set in front of the basin's blue-and-white tile walls.

Meat and milk crocks are stored in the basin.

Through a second sluice on the other end of the three-meter-long basin, the original force of the current is restored to the mountain stream; it flows on between the wooden posts that support the straw roof.

The customers say that at one time the café owner bred rare species of fish in the cooling basin; the colorful fish swam back and forth among the meat and milk crocks, supposedly nibbling the algae out of the joints of the tile walls.

But then, the customers continue, the café owner gave up fish breeding because it was no longer worth the trouble, just for the few customers who wanted to eat fish. Formerly, in better times, however, tell the customers, one supposedly could eat a variety of fish, black or colored fish, and in the mountains it smelled of fish being broiled on a spit over a charcoal fire by the café owner.

On the rock wall above the stove hang four tapestries showing gray and red heads in mountain scenes and many cafés built into rock

and two photographs with the faces of the great-grandfather and his son, the grandfather of the present-day café owner, framed, fastened to the rock with iron studs and hooks; and it is said that the present-day café owner has already had himself photographed and the picture framed so that one day, when his son takes over the café, the son of the present-day café owner, being a respectable café owner, would then hang his picture, that of the present-day café owner, next to the other two pictures on which the faces of the great-grandfather and his son, the grandfather of the present-day café owner, can be seen.

The people say there are, of course, many other cafés in the area, built years ago, with dome-shaped roofs, where in front of the entrances you can still see old wooden stands stained with tallow, riding animals having been tied to them at one time. These are said to be two wooden poles rising vertically two meters out of the ground with iron hooks screwed into their tops; the reins of the riding animals supposedly were hitched to them.

Above the entrance doors of these establishments the following proverb could often still be read:

FOR THE MOST PART ONE GOES MUCH MORE WITH THE TIMES

BY GOING AGAINST THE TIMES

IN RECENT TIMES IT HAS

BECOME COMMON PRACTICE

TO GO AGAINST THE TIMES

SO THAT IN THE END THE GOING-AGAINST-THE-TIMES

HAS AGAIN BECOME A GOING-WITH-THE-TIMES

THAT IS WHY RECENTLY SOME ARE GOING WITH THE TIMES

IN THE ORIGINAL SENSE OF THE IDEA
ONLY TO ACTUALLY GO AGAINST THE TIMES
IN THEIR VERY OWN WAY
AND THEREBY ABOVE ALL
IN THE END TO MORE EASILY GO WITH THE TIMES AGAIN.

—*The village square is empty.*
—*We can walk across the village square.*
—*People are sitting in the café.*
—*Let's walk across the village square.*
—*The village square is empty.*

No, that's not true, because
the village square is f l o o d e d; the water flows through the cracks of the
closed doors into the corridors, halls, vestibules, and cellars, has filled the
cellars, stands one meter deep; the people glide over it, across it, in boats,
skiffs converging up front at sharp angles; the figures stand upright in their
boats, hold meters-long poles in their hands, push them onto the ground of
the village square lying one meter below the water level, push themselves
off, move ahead, cross the square, go from house to house supplying each
other with food, fuel, sayings, and rumors, several also wear boots that
reach to their hips and wade to the other side; conversations sparkle in the
rippling waves that are drawn on the surface by the wind; boats, standing
and walking figures, steps and poles are reproduced upside down by the
reflecting surface of the water; the figures push the poles through the water
onto the pavement visible beneath the reflection, sometimes they lay the
poles inside the boats, call to each other, enjoy the rain, tell jokes, they're
used to keeping their sense of humor in any situation in life, they supply
each other with food, sayings, fuel, and rumors, have reached a front door;
from the inside, its wings, pushed outward, move the water aside; waves
slap against the walls on the other side; packages are tossed into the black
interior of the houses, packages are received from the black interior of the
houses, are tossed into the cargo space of the skiff; push off from the facades with the poles, go on; the figures have to be careful so that the boats
don't capsize from hitting too hard against the well winch crossbar just

above the water; conversations and laughter sparkle in the rippling waves, they're used to keeping their sense of humor in any situation in life, enjoy the rain; the village square is flooded, the people glide over it, across it in boats; you can hear the poles hitting into the ground beneath the reflection of the water's surface, or one wears boots that reach to one's hips and wades through.

—*It must have rained for a long time.*

—*The sewers must have been clogged up.*

—*No, they drowned in the rain, couldn't hold any more water, overflowed.*

—*The water's escape routes out of the village must have been blocked.*

—*The water couldn't drain away.*

—*The village square flooded.*

    yes i remember earlier heard a rustling in the air turned around saw the man as he entered the common of the village swung his walking stick in the air really pushed it into the ground let it swing back and forth pushed it into the ground then he let the stick swing out so far that the tip traced a big semicircle with his fist closed around the handle as its center and touched the sky really stuck into the clouds thrust into the firmament poked around in the laundry room of all the smoggy horizon's cathedral naves bent his elbows downward until the tip of the stick again on the ground

    behind the walls in the yards the people had planted shrubs in the narrow streets the doors opened halfway in the door cracks heads and pairs of eyes became visible through the slits of the door cracks i was able to divine the interior of the houses and yards

fire
shrub
fans
then

the doors closed again and the man entered the village square walked to the well leaned his walking stick against the brick-patterned wall of the well turned the crank of the well winch hoisted the bucket from the depth of the well and stooped drank water from the hollow of his hand holding his face over the bucket which was reproducing the clouds

yes i remember quite clearly again put his fingers around the stick's handle once more thrust the walking stick into the sky spit out unintelligible words syllables of a strange unknown language the people stood behind the closed windows holding their hands in front of their faces only once in a while looked through their fingers spread in front of their eyes through the windowpanes at the stranger in front of the well waving his stick around in the sky put all their hope in the priest thought he would at any moment come running with a cross in his hand hold the cross in front of the face of the man at the well

no the handle of the rectory door wasn't pressed down the door wings didn't open the priest didn't come running with fluttering robes held the cross neither in his hands nor in front of the man's face but rather opened the rectory office window which looks out to the village square yes i saw that he walked to the bookshelf on the wall opposite the window from the top shelf took down the village chronicle carried it to the desk opened it took pen in hand and began to write

A man came into the village; he drank from our well, pointed with the tip of his stick into the sky, turned his face toward the clouds; threatening looks appeared on it as if they had been cast into his eyes by the weather. He spoke a strange language; I wasn't able to write down his words because his speech could have been mistaken for the cawing of seven ravens; immediately thereafter I ordered the cook to put the soup kettle on the fire, walked out to the village square, and tried to make clear to the stranger at the well that he was invited in; stood in front of him imitating the motions of eating with my hand so that he might understand me; guided my right hand to my mouth, the tips of my thumb, index finger, and middle finger joined as if I were holding the handle of a spoon or other eating utensil between my fingers; then I pointed to the rectory, gesturing to the stranger that he should come along; I reached my arms up into the air in front of me and back again, and turned my face toward the stranger, who pushed his stick into the ground and looked at me; then I turned around and took the first inviting steps from the well to the rectory door in the hope that he would follow me, his host; but he didn't follow me; I didn't hear any steps behind me; when I had reached the rectory door, I turned around and saw him still standing next to the well; I then walked back to him once more, repeated the described gestures, once more reached my hands into the air and back again, once more walked invitingly ahead to the rectory door, again turned around in front of the door in the hope that he followed me this time; but again I was mistaken, because, while I was walking to the house, he must have turned around and taken the direction opposite the one I suggested, walking to the right, past the town hall; before I had opened the door, I saw him take the road to the elongated trapezoid mountains. Rather than accept, he declined my invitation. When his figure reached the first rocks of the mountains, his silhouette, visible only as a point, cast behind it two one-kilometer-long shadows, which touched the first roofs of the village in the west: skin shadow and stick shadow.

When the stranger had disappeared into the mountains, clouds darkened the hollow surrounding the village. Several people lit candles and small gas lamps in their rooms. Then it began to rain. Strings of water formed straight lines from the sky to the meadows, roofs, narrow streets, fences, and to the ground of the village square. The ropes of water, on which a much-too-early dusk tied to them is descending, struck the stone pavement of the square and were tossed far back into the foggy air. The impact produced brass-colored sparks because the drops reflected the yellow lights behind the window crosses. Then a few clouds changed into rocks and mud and fell down from the mountains, breaking into the hollow of the valley. The stream bed clogged up, the village square flooded, some huts along the edge of the village were buried.

The people of the village then remembered the stranger, yes, one should have interpreted his stick movements in the sky as a warning of the flood, should have understood his strange incantations as prophecies.

On the other side of the mountains, it was said to be even worse. It is said the mud totally covered the villages. You could still hear voices from sunken roofs beneath the planet's skin. The people say they also saw the stranger with his stick in other villages on the other side of the mountains. There, too, he is said to have spurned all hospitality and traveled on into the mountains. E v e r y w h e r e   a t   e x a c t l y   t h e   s a m e   t i m e.   But the possibility of mirages and hallucinations is also being considered.

You said
—*let's walk across the village square;*
—*we can't walk across the village square,*
I retorted,
—*because the village square is flooded.*
The people go across the village square by boat; the water runs off; the mud dries, crumbles out of the joints; they get brooms out of the storerooms and cellars, sweep narrow streets and walls, climb onto the roofs, sweep the tiles; the wind blows the gray mud dust swirling in the air back into the mountains; you can hear the scratching of bristles in the gutters, see figures standing on their balconies, swaying their chests, arms, hands holding broomsticks, and bottoms back and forth and up and down.

Corrugated Iron and Door

In the evening the corrugated iron is rolled down.

In the morning it is rolled up again, disappearing into a cast-iron slot in the wall above the upper door frame and presumably rolling up,

this can almost be taken for granted,

between the bricks in the interior of the wall not visible to the onlooker. The corrugated iron is gray like the gray of dawn east of the village. The people in the village say the reason the corrugated iron is so gray is that every day the gray of dawn from the east touches the corrugated iron and lends it its color. The corrugated iron, say the people, has stolen its color from the gray of dawn and put it between the iron grooves.

In the glass sections of the door you can see the reflection of the well.

When the door is slowly opened, you can see the reflection of the well,

divided by a ten-centimeter-wide wooden board leading vertically from the upper rail of the door to the lower door section, which is one and a half meters high and one meter wide,

slip slowly away from the glass;

it appears as if the reflection of the well were moving into the wall of the house or directly into the room located behind the door, but that's an error on your part because only the door's glass is escaping the reflection, and the reflection is preserved in the air between the door-frame posts, invisible to your retina;

and, when you see the door slowly close again, you can see the well reflection moving toward the door's glass; at first you see only small portions, then half of the reflected brick wall of the well; then the reflected winch slowly becomes visible;

and it appears as if the reflected well were moving from the wall of the house or from the interior of the room toward the glass, but that's an error on your part because the reflection of the well built of brick, invisible to your retina, has always been trapped in the air on the same spot between the door-frame posts, and only now, because you see someone very slowly closing the door, can you see how the reflection of the well again becomes visible on the glass because the door's glass has taken up the spot in the air between the door-frame posts.

It moves, the glass sections between the wooden boards shake, the reflected crank of the winch sways.

The glass set in the door was poorly pressed at the glassworks, has irregularities that distort the reflected well, the lines of the brick pattern appear wavy.

When the door is quickly opened and closed you think you are catching a brief glimpse of a gray patch of shadow,

which, however, you don't seem to remember having seen earlier, but only simultaneous with the quick opening of the door,

escaping from the wall and falling out from it between the door frames. That is the power of your retina's imagination, having become accustomed to the presence of the reflection and seeking an explanation for its sudden disappearance. The process is too quick for your brain; you think you are seeing a gray shadow shaking on the wall, disappearing, appearing, and disappearing again. Yes, your brain explains this process to you, which, due to its speed, is momentarily puzzling, with this gray patch of shadow, whose contours are blurred, barely visible.

The Trees

The trees are hollow inside.
This tree has been opened up by someone.
In the hollow of the trunk someone started a fire.
Smoke is rising from the treetop now.
But also from all the other treetops, knotholes and injured bark of the
ornate trees that have grown in an entirely baroque style in this area,
whose r o o t s a r e c o n n e c t e d w i t h e a c h o t h e r under the
ground by silver hoses.

The Village Square

—The village square is empty.
—We can walk across the village square.
—The flies' chitins are hissing in the limy walls.
—Let's walk across the village square.
—The laundry is drying on the roofs above the bathrooms;
—red sheets with gray zigzagged borders are hanging on the lines.
—The village square is empty.
—The wood wasp is seeking out the tile pattern.
—Behind the village, the brickworks.

Behind the roof of the brickworks, the brickworks owner. With his hammer he pounds bricks out of the mountain. The rock is brick red. The brickworks owner puts the bricks on the kiln. Out of the smokestack, one hundred meters away from the brickworks, brick-red smoke.
Take the hammer out of the brickworks owner's hand and read the word

DIKE

off the tool's four flat surfaces which are not touched by the rock during the hammering, separated, quartered, four-sided, smooth
into:

75

Fig. 5

on each nonstriking side of the hammer a letter of the word.

On top of the smokestack the brickworks owner has mounted an iron pole. The smokestack is thirty meters high.

The brickworks owner drove in forty-five iron rungs. Iron rung above iron rung. While he stood on the iron rung two-iron-rung lengths below the iron rung just driven in, he drove in a new iron rung one-iron-rung length above the iron rung just driven in.

He climbed up the smokestack. Above his head his hands clawed around the iron rung above him, his soles on the iron rung below him, in this way he climbed up the smokestack and mounted an iron pole on top of the smokestack, with his hammer he knocked a hole into the stone of the smokestack between the outside air and the thirty-two-meter-high cylinder of smokestack air;

the knocked-out stones fell through the smokestack air thirty-two meters below the top of the smokestack;

I heard the stones falling inside the smokestack, their hissing in the smokestack air, their striking against the sooty inside walls and the bottom of the smokestack,

76

I saw the stones falling down outside the smokestack, their impact, after the impact, their repeated bouncing back up to half the height of the smokestack, fifteen meters, their final shattering at the foot of the smokestack;

earlier, however, some, while they were still in the air, had changed into quick birds, flying into the horizon situated sixty meters behind it, while the brickworks owner stood on top of the smokestack, computed the free fall formula using height, time, and gravitation, set the pole into the knocked-out hole, climbed down again, mixed mortar in the brickworks behind the dusty windows by candle and brick kiln light; I saw the fire behind the black windows, behind the dusty windows, which some boys had broken in his absence, the shattered pieces lie next to the wall; the air is an infinite geometric progression, the clatter of glass panes falling into pieces is reproduced by the air in specific time intervals according to the laws of an infinite geometric progression, you will again be able to hear, in I-don't-know-how-many years, the striking and hissing of the stones in the smokestack, a bit later the clatter of panes breaking into pieces;

the brickworks owner climbed up the smokestack again, in one hand the bucket full of mortar, above his head his other hand clawed around the iron rung above his hair, then up there he poured the mortar into the hole that earlier had been knocked out of the top of the smokestack wall, rammed, wedged, fastened the pole between stones, bricks, in the wet mortar; the smokestack is blackened, from the top a parabola whose curve is pointing toward the ground,

on the pole over the top of the smokestack flutters the flag with the mayor's picture.

The smokestack is located one hundred meters away from the brickworks. It is not connected with the brickworks, nor with the kiln that is in the brickworks building. Although the brickworks smoke rises out of it into the sky which is suspended each day forty meters above the ground.

But this, obviously, is a common error.

Because the connecting pipes are laid underground.

The stranger who comes to the brickworks sees the brickworks and the smokestack, which is connected with it invisibly and, therefore, in his opinion, not connected with it at all, but is smoking nonetheless, the stranger, not knowing this, is astonished. And the people of the village often make fun of the astonished strangers, joking about the fact that underground pipes don't occur to them, because people are generally of the firm conviction that everyone's intellectual faculties ought to have been far enough developed to come to suspect,

because it is in no way evident, an underground connection between the brickworks building and the smokestack, because, aided by his native intelligence, one would say to himself, the smoke, after all, would have to flow into the smokestack from somewhere, and it couldn't just smoke out of the ground into the smokestack. The brickworks owner dug a trench between the smokestack and the brickworks building underneath the brickworks wall facing the smokestack all the way to the kiln, laid iron pipes in it, cemented, welded, soldered them together, diverted the kiln pipe from the top of the kiln through the chimney, but connected the chimney flue with the pipes in the trench, on the other side connected the other end of the pipe run with the beginning of the smokestack's interior two meters below the ground at the foot of the smokestack, filled up the trench.

Transparent smoke is now rising out of the smokestack.

The air above the smokestack is quivering.

The mayor's face on the flag is getting black cheeks from the smoke.

You can follow the path of the trench between the brickworks wall facing the smokestack and the smokestack, follow the general direction of the rocks on top of the sandy backfill among the well established scabious and the burs floating gently above them, whose lanterns twinkle like fireflies throughout the afternoon.

The gate to the brickworks is a romanesque arch.

—*We can walk across the village square.*
—*Let's walk across the village square.*
—*The village square is empty.*

No, that's not true, because
the c o n s c r i p t i o n   d e t a c h m e n t has come into the village, in the village square I see the row of lined-up soldiers.

yes i remember earlier i heard a drumming in the ground then behind us the steps rolled down the hill i turned around perceived the glistening of the bayonets and saw the soldiers as they entered the common of the village the major in front behind him the master sergeant then on the meadow behind us they took off their backpacks untied the sausagelike tent rolls from their backpacks unrolled them hung black triangles into the horizon laid them together to form black circles drove wooden stakes into the soil beneath the ether where black tents were pitched whose dark holes swallowed up everyone while the major walked across the village square and disappeared in the town hall

behind the walls in the yards the people had planted shrubs in the narrow streets the doors opened halfway in the door cracks heads and pairs of eyes appeared through the slits of the door cracks i was able to divine the interior of the houses and yards
                                    fire
                                        shrub
                                            fans
                                                then the
door wings clapped shut again and the soldiers crawled out of their tents later the doors opened again the people flocked out of the walls with kith and kin filled the narrow streets stood at the walls where the main roads flow into the village square

INSIGHT:

TYPICAL CHARACTERISTICS OF TENT DWELLERS:
PEOPLE LIE IN THE TENT;
HOWEVER, WHEN THEY RISE,
THEIR BACKS BRUSH AGAINST THE INSIDE TENT CANVAS;
THE PEOPLE IN FRONT OF THE TENT REALIZE,
FROM A FAMILIAR RUSTLING OF THE TENT CANVAS,
THAT THOSE WHO ARE INSIDE THE TENT HAVE RISEN
AND MAKE THE NECESSARY PREPARATIONS.

I see the row of soldiers lined up in the village square. Then the door of the town hall opens, the major comes out with the mayor, the master sergeant, facing the soldiers in a military manner, commands

—*Detachment, attention!* the soldiers stand at attention, the major walks with the mayor toward the row of lined-up soldiers, the master sergeant commands

—*Detachment, eyes right!* the soldiers turn to face the major and the mayor, move their faces along the path of the two, the master sergeant, in a military manner, turns to the major, who has also come to the position of attention, the mayor stands alongside, master sergeant and major salute, the master sergeant bellows at the major

—*Sir, the conscription detachment is all present and accounted for in the village square!*

the major replies —*thank you, commence,*

master sergeant and major salute, the master sergeant again turns toward the soldiers, shouts

—*Detachment, attention! Detachment, commence!* whereupon the soldiers, after starting to march in a pounding parade step, disperse at a run throughout the village in a star-shaped pattern.

All the people of the village have gathered in the square, on its edges along the four lines of house facades, they are angry; I can hear their grumbling and muttering

—*just let 'em come in for a big surprise that's the limit that's too much nothin' but girls on their minds take away workers but chase skirts and just let 'em search and this time though hide the young boys real good.*

Gradually the soldiers have come back to the village square again; they had gone into houses, down into cellars, into the church behind the altar, threw open cupboards, closets, commodes and sideboards, overturned empty and full barrels, dug through wood and coal, broke open barn doors, scattered the straw on the threshing floors, shone lights under beds, rummaged in blankets, scattered haystacks, looked into the well, wrecked the order of the bookcases, searched for small underground rooms, discovered seams and traces of trapdoors, found ten young lads, dragged them to the village square by the collar. A soldier has gotten table and chair from the inn, has set them up, takes out a book, opens it up, sits down, begins to write, has them give their names, and a medic examines the physical condition of the lads by tapping them on their shoulders with his hand; the major is satisfied, says

—*they'll be fine soldiers someday.*

All the people have gathered on the square, on its edges along the four lines of house facades, they are angry; I can hear their grumbling and muttering —*not enough workers stupid soldiers nothin' but screwin' and fuckin' on their minds but in their brains nothin' but straw so much it sticks outta their skulls and then in the barracks from behind 'cause there's nobody else 'round and then the officers with the boys from the village and seduce.*

yes i remember later i again heard a drumming in the ground and then behind us the steps rolled down on the other side of the hill turned around saw the soldiers dissolve with the lads in the horizon

crest

fence

     sign

then the people again withdrew into the walls with kith and kin disappeared between the cracks in the door wings

hair

window

wood

General and Specific Economic Measures

1.

The successful individual is righteous before God.
Lately, a lot of canals are being built here.
Slowly but surely, a changeover in fuel from charcoal to hard coal is taking place.
Until now, the iron industry has used nothing but charcoal.
There are no longer enough forests.
Soon, however, we will have at our disposal the canals necessary for transporting coal.
Bulk goods are heavy, the use of rivers and waterways inexpensive.
No one need be ashamed of being in business.

2.

Irrigation system for fields and gardens:
On both sides of the roads between rows of trees fifty centimeters apart from each other, flow forty-centimeter-wide and twenty-five-centimeter-deep streams along the sides of the fields and gardens,
in front of each ditch, a wooden sluice shaped like a trapezoid, the shorter side of it down, in a wooden guide, above the center of the longer side facing up, a wooden stick, a lever to put your hand on, for opening or closing the sluice.
In the ditches in the ground the soil is smooth from the effect of the water running between the plants and trees, dried mud, d r i e d   u p   p a t c h-e s   o f   w a t e r   along the edges;

between the rows of trees verdigris grows on the bark; several trunks stand right in the water, the wood has turned black from the c o n t i n u o u s t w i l i g h t between the rows of trees fifty centimeters apart from each other.

3.
Irrigation system for a walled-in area:

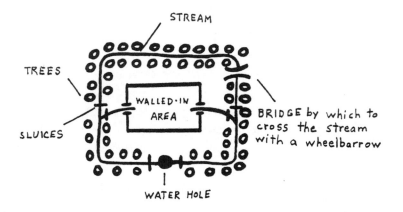

Fig. 6

The stream flows out of a circular water hole lying level with the ground. By means of pipes passing under the wall one can let the stream flow into the enclosed area in two places.

However, the possibility also exists not to let the stream get into the interior of the walled-in area at all but, rather, to set the sluice wings in such a way that in time the entire walled-in area is at first surrounded by a moat of water; soon the stream overflows the moat's bank and all of the land nearby and farther away is covered with a s k i n o f w a t e r.

4.

Dairy farming

*The old butter churns have begun to leak so much, especially around the
turning gears, that sometimes the milk or the not-quite-ready cream or the
not-quite-ready butter drips on the floor in the butter churn rooms.*
*Then on the floor the milk turns into curds, and for weeks the curd and
cream spots that have dried up there can be admired.*
Consequence:
*the worms and maggots are lured out of the joints, boards, and walls, eat
the traces of dried milk off the floors of the musty and moldy-smelling butter churn rooms.*
This is an untenable situation!
*In the future strong measures will have to be taken with regard to the mold
on the walls.*
*It will soon be necessary to take a very sharp knife in one's right hand and
with it scrape the mold off the walls of the butter churn rooms.*
It'll really come trickling down then!
Later we'll talk about the acquisition of new butter churns.

The Village Square

—The village square is empty.
—Except for the well in the center, I see nothing in the village square.
—Let's walk across the village square.

The stone slabs on the ground end at the walls of the houses, at the beginning of the visible cellar walls, which are ten centimeters wider than the actual house walls. The visible cellar walls are one meter high, cemented gray; the house walls made of brick begin on top of them; the cellars are wider than the houses; that's why on the facades, at the height of one meter, ten-centimeter-wide, level ledges run corner to corner all the way around.
The children bowl their hoops across the square, run along behind the rolling hoops, catch up with them, push them farther on with a stick so that they roll far ahead of them.
On the stone I hear the screeching of these wobbling hoops made of rusty iron. Sometimes one of them falls over if it is hit wrong with the stick, falls over, continues wobbling on the stone ground for a long time.
The hoop lies still, is put upright again, bowled, pushed, chased in a circle around the well in the village square.
Sometimes I see windows open. Angry looks between the window frames, people who are irritated by the noise, *inconsiderate, noise, quiet down, complain, can't stand, put an end to, prohibit, cover your ears, not possible, inconsiderate.*
The children brush their hands atop the cellar walls, running along beside, let their iron hoop bowling sticks slide along the wall ledges, while the dust

86

pushed by the sticks flies out of the joints and is carried away by the wind.

I see the cellar windows in the projecting cellar foundations. The cellars are deep; you can walk down, will see that they are as deep as the houses are high; their windows are partly barred, the glass is dusty.

I see wagons coming with tree trunks, coal, and cut firewood. The tree trunks reach beyond the shoulders of the horses into the white air. In front of and next to the heads of the animals you can see the two-year-old cut surfaces. If you were to walk by, the driver would ask you to tell him offhand how many annual rings there are. You would owe him an answer until the next time.

The cellar windows open; wood and coal are dumped in front, are pushed with shovels through the open windows into the depth. I can hear the skidding of the shovels, while the wagons leave the village, the singing of the ungreased axles between the wheels. Wood and coal disappear in the windows, whose wings clap shut; the panes are dusty from the heaps of coal that have plunged by them into the cellar abysses and have already fallen asleep; it is almost impossible to look down through the dirty wire glass; you can only see when someone from the house climbs down with you and turns on the light in the rooms.

Fruit is stored, preserved in jars; the people need potatoes over the winter; there are likely to be pears on the racks or quinces set side by side in single rows one above the other, and the pumpkins roll through the shelves into another area of the eternal nights locked up in the depths; the nights' gray of dawn sometimes protests, climbs up, steps up to the window frames and shakes them until it soon sinks down again, exhausted, having changed into dusk.

—*We can walk across the village square.*
—*Yes, let's walk across the village square.*
—*The village square is empty with the exception of the well in the center.*

No, that's not true, because I see d u g - u p   t r e e   s t u m p s lying around; they lie along the edges of the square next to the walls of the houses; see their huge roots, root clusters, dirt still clinging to them, clods of dirt in the center of the spherical, two-meter-wide root systems, next to them the holes in the ground, deep cavities from which the roots were torn out. The loosened stone slabs near the excavations.

A short time ago workers must have been here, lifted off the stone slabs around the stumps, begun to dig, dug under the roots, tied them with ropes, together pulled them out, *heave ho, all together, really, watch it, stop, let go, no, heave ho, all together.*

They dug out all the roots, slipped off into the barns, lay down in the hay, slept.

I see them enter the village square from the narrow side streets. The last one leads a horse by the halter, one holds a thick hemp rope in his hands.

The horse has a harness on its shoulders that glistens in the sun, pulls a beam along behind, one and a half meters long; its ends are connected to the harness by long leather straps, it has been ferruled with iron, it skids behind; I hear the irregular clanking of the ferrules on the village square pavement.

They go to the first dug-up stump, tie the hemp rope around the root ball, then to the beam; the horse pulls the root along behind it through a narrow street to the edge of the village, the workers along behind, *gee up, giddyap, pull, go, get out, go on, gee up, giddyap.*

Not much time goes by, they come back with the horse, the ferruled iron sections of the skidding beam sing in the joints of the pavement. They tie on the second root, the horse pulls it out of the village, I hear their whistles while they trot along behind the animal, sometimes they sing a song in four-four time, the whip cracks, the towed roots leave brown dirt trails on the white stone, *faster, okay, boring, tie, pull, get finished, take time, okay, faster.*

Then all the roots are gone, a wagon full of dirt appears, the dirt is dumped into the holes, gravel on top, stones joined together with mixed mortar, the white slabs pounded into the ground with sledge hammers, the blows repeated by the house walls as echoes.

Perhaps it's noon by now.

The village square is quickly cleaned with hot water, soap powder added beforehand; they take rags, wet the pavement, scrub the stones with brushes, *clean, spick-and-span, nicer, spotless, really, brush, wipe, clean, spick-and-span.*

They take all their stuff, leave the square by way of the narrow streets through which they came, sit down to snack at the edge of the village, take their bread and sausage out of its newspaper wrapping.

Perhaps it's noon by now.

The stones glisten, the pavement is still wet from the cleaning up, the traces of rags wiped back and forth can still be followed.

Folk Song

Very lively

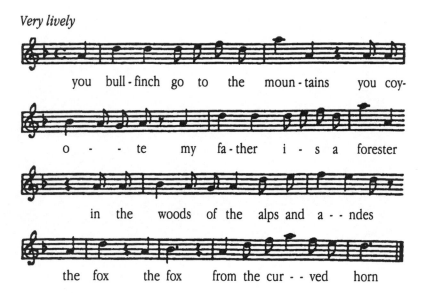

you bull - finch go to the moun - tains you coy-

o - - te my fa - ther i - s a forester

in the woods of the alps and a - - ndes

the fox the fox from the cur - - ved horn

The Village Square

—Now the village square is empty.
—Except for the well in the center, there is nothing in the village square.
—We can walk across the village square.
—You're right.
—Let's walk across the village square.
—The village square is empty.

No, that's not true, because there are b e n c h e s set up on the edges of the square, their backs turned toward the walls;
long before the people had sat on the tree stumps; the tree stumps had been torn out, so they couldn't sit in the village square anymore, were angry, *no longer sit, not fair, what nerve, complain, nothing done, incompetent, mismanagement, poor planning, not fair, no longer sit.*
The community council was understanding, by unanimous decision in its meeting promised replacements, *public health, beautification, improvement, upgrading of education, emergency relief, recreational activity, satisfaction, beautification, public health.*
Then from the city came wagons on which the benches were shipped. The two drivers of each wagon unloaded them, set them up on the edges of the square, the backs of the benches turned toward the walls.
Drivers have whips, leather aprons, gray scarfs on their hair with black tassels hanging over their shoulders, and dark faces; I heard them grumbling while working, *rough road, bumpy, asinine, all for nothing anyway, why do these yokels need benches, heavy, bumpy, idiot, blockhead.*

91

I saw them in the east behind a hill, traveling down the horizon. Then they dropped down from the last visible skyline which they had reached until nothing was left to be seen of them.

They are benches from the city, like the ones they set up there in parks, tree-lined streets, public grounds, gardens, and boulevards, benches with colorful pieces of wood; the surfaces of the wooden boards and the ornamented cast iron underneath are coated with green oil paint. On the backrests, under the light that falls on the square, glistens the anticipated joy that reflects off the surfaces where people customarily sit down.

There are benches set up on the edges, on which people sit; they look at each other, look at the passersby, and the passersby look back at those sitting.

We had hidden in the blacksmith's workshop, cheeks pressed up against the walls; no one saw us, and you said

—*let's walk across the village square;*

—*no, let's not walk across the village square,*

I replied, because I saw the p e o p l e sitting on the b e n c h e s, two on each bench.

We couldn't walk across the village square because we weren't supposed to be seen, and we observed how those sitting on the benches c o u l d n ' t see us, because we didn't walk across the village square; we saw how they d i d n ' t see us.

—*Let's walk across the village square anyhow.*

—*We can't walk across the village square,*

I said once more, because some figures wearing work clothes turned up, twice as many as there were benches, two went to each bench, politely asking the figures sitting on the benches to rise by gesturing with their hands, *please, get up, go away, have to, ordered, from above, don't be angry, please, get up.*

The sitting figures rose in astonishment, casting each other questioning hand gestures, which were answered in turn with baffled looks, expressions and motions of ignorance, *what for, outrageous, what nerve, here we go again, won't stand for, complain, bring charges, raise a protest, file an appeal, show them, outrageous, the limit, what for.*

They withdrew into their houses; I heard their indignant slamming of doors.

Those in work clothes carried away the benches, two to a bench, from the village square to the edge of the village, there set them up in a row on a meadow. Then I found out it had something to do with the b i r d s which may come again. The people whispered apprehensively, hid in their houses, *birds peck out all the lime mortar, walls ruined, damage bricks, fall out, eat away plaster, houses collapse, birds, peck out all the lime mortar.* The mayor convened the community council, made a speech before the assembled people.

—When the birds came for the first time, many years ago, all the people were helpless, hid in their houses, closed the windows, looked out the windows apprehensively, drew the curtains; the birds dived from the sky shrieking loudly; one had to cover his ears, no one could stand their high-pitched song; the animals dived at the walls, held fast with their claws in the joints and poked their beaks into the walls like mad; all the plaster was eaten up; then they disappeared into the sky again, a huge flock; their feathers are white, so that in the white air the outline of their bodies can barely be seen, almost transparent; one can detect their presence only by a vigorous, fast flapping around in the air or violently descending vibrations on the skin of the tightly stretched sky above; when they claw themselves into the walls, the dimension of their bodies can be estimated: the smallest ones barely bigger than a wren or a hummingbird, the larger ones, however, can reach the size of ravens, of crows, sometimes easily the size of falcons, and not infrequently even the size of vultures.
Years ago, when such a flock descended upon us for the first time, no one did anything about it; everyone was afraid, after the collapse of the walls, they expected to be chopped to pieces just like them; most of them had hidden deep down in their cellar storerooms, in the deepest bottoms of their potato bins, or buried themselves in the heaps of coal, and not until a few hours after the flock had again flown away did the first people dare to venture out; all the houses stood completely bare, as if the brickwork had never been plastered over; between the bricks the animals had pecked, hacked, eaten out all the lime mortar, but not a single brick; nevertheless, all the walls fell apart. Time passed, we soon forgot all about it; the houses were freshly plastered and repaired.

In the following year, at the same time, many say to the exact hour and minute, it all happened again; and even then there were a few who bravely left their houses, tried to chase the birds away from the walls with sticks, brooms, and shovels; however, they wouldn't let themselves be chased away, but with lightning speed avoided the whacks, quite badly ate away the walls, as if the houses had been dipped in acid, and not a single bird was killed; in many cases the damage was worse than the first time; even more walls collapsed, many holes had been eaten through the walls in the houses.

It couldn't go on this way, people then realized that the village would collapse every year when the birds eat the mortar and lime out of the walls or peck and hack it out with their beaks. A single house remained practically untouched then; I ask you, over there, as you knew I would, to tell us about it again.

—It was a coincidence, because I was just watering my garden then, when the birds came and began attacking my walls too; because I was terribly startled by the singing cries of the animals falling from the sky, and as I was being enveloped by the frightful screams of the fluttering song of this cloud of flashing, beaming, feathered wings wildly flapping around me, I accidentally sprayed the walls of the house with the garden hose instead of spraying the garden, but immediately saw, to my surprise, that the animals, as if trying to escape, flew away in a flash from those sections of the walls which, by chance at first, were being hit with the water jet from the hose; afraid of water, I then thought to myself, the fowl sense a dangerous threat from the water, and I kept spraying my house; for that reason only very little damage was done.

—I thank you; we learned from this, in following years took precautions, acquired many garden hoses from the city, then we stood in front of the houses and s p r a y e d the fowl d o w n from the walls until the flock, exhausted, withdrew into the sky, the cloud of birds flew away again. Once we equipped scientists, zoologists, a few people with blowguns, crossbows, pistols, carbines, air guns, Flobert rifles, shotguns, machine guns, etc., positioned them throughout the village, hoping to shoot down a few animals

so that a more detailed analysis as to which species, for example, could be conducted with the aid of specimens; but the people did not hit a single animal with their weapons, they say they kept shooting their weapons in continuous fire as they aimed at the flapping in the air, at the barely visible bodies behind the scarcely detectable beaks of the winged animals; even the birds that clawed themselves into the walls, which were thought to be easier to hit, sure shots, easily dodged the fast projectiles of the rifles and pistols, and afterwards only the bullet holes in walls could still be seen, and nothing was caught in the ingeniously devised and expertly camouflaged bird traps on the roofs and walls.

As much as he regretted it, the zoologist said, in this case, even he, as a zoologist and a natural scientist, was completely powerless and at his wits' end.

That's why we still don't know what we are fighting but do have at our disposal the most effective method, *w a t e r , s p r a y i n g w a t e r o u t o f h o s e s ,* like the fire brigade. Once the flock came unexpectedly in the middle of the night screaming out of the darkness with its unbearable song, assaulting our stunned dreams, because we weren't prepared, again caused great damage. Since then, we always keep ourselves and everything ready; guards are posted to sound the alarm when the dangerous singing in the air softly rises far away and the screaming comes closer and closer, soon enveloping our heads from above.

The figures in work clothes carried away the benches; that has something to do with the birds that will be coming.

—*Nothing must block the walls; the benches, I had them hauled from the village square so that they wouldn't cover up the house walls behind them, nothing in the way, just as everything else standing around and lying around the houses had to be moved so that, at any time that the screaming song of the enveloping bird cloud shreds our thoughts, we have a clear view enabling us to completely protect every spot on every one of the walls surrounding us.*

The New Law

The new law is being posted on all barn walls. Striking hammers drive the nails through the paper made from reeds into the wood. When the points of the nails pierce the paper at the edges, the white fibers rustle. There's a hissing before the nail, hit by the hammer blow, penetrates the barn wood. You can see billposters' hands holding hammers; they position the nails before hitting them, standing on one leg in front of the wooden brown walls, the other leg raised, pulled up, so that the kneecap presses the lower edge of the poster against the wall, as they drive the first nail through one of the two upper corners of the notice into the wood; they then stand on both legs in front of it, pressing one of their arms against the not-yet-fastened upper edge of the paper to make sure that the sheet hangs straight, comparing the border of the top section of the poster with the line of the barn roof's overhang; only then is a second nail driven through the other upper corner; then the billposter takes two steps back so that he can visually assess, with a critical eye, the potential public effect of the announcement on the barn wall; then he steps back up to the wall, takes two more nails out of the pouch lying at his feet and drives them through the two lower corners of the official notice into the barn wood; while he is doing this, you can usually find him in a stooped or half-bowed position, his bottom covered by the billposter's uniform trousers material, swaying back and forth to the rhythm of the blows, to the left and to the right.

Billposters are usually full-bearded people with wire-rimmed glasses, various types of physician's bags, climbing boots, woolen kneesocks, knickers, knapsacks with strapped-on ice axes, felt hats with pheasant, grouse, partridge, or chicken feathers and mountain climber's gear pinned on, who turn up in the remotest parts of the land, are greeted happily by the children because they often give them bent nails, crumpled paper scraps, stretched-out rubber kneebands, discarded rusty hinges in various sizes, torn suspenders, broken-off pieces of barbed wire, and many other things, but have to watch out that the posters they carry rolled up under their arms aren't stolen.

When barn walls aren't available, he nails the announcement on trees, pigsties, benches, farmhouses, grain silos, or chalets; if, in the last case, he happens to disturb a dairymaid, waking her from her sleep if it's early, she awakened by the hammering opens the window right away, waves, and gives a friendly smile.

The New Law:
For reasons of security it will henceforth be prohibited to walk through forests and along tree-lined roads in order to protect the population from the b l a c k   m e n   who hide so well in the shadows of the trees that sometimes they can hardly be distinguished from the darkness of the tree-lined roads. It is the intention of judicial authorities that the people, who from now on will move   o n l y   i n   t h e   o p e n   c o u n t r y s i d e ,   can be i m-m e d i a t e l y   d i s c o v e r e d   and categorized by the personnel, geodesists, surveyors, constables, soldiers, and their assistants, who are responsible for their sector of observation; people who come across the   h o r i-z o n   into their sector of observation can quickly be plotted, registered, and classified, two or three times; prior to the time of the new law, despite all deliberate efforts, such thoroughness was never possible, indeed, sometimes not enforceable at all, because the people almost always walked through forests and along tree-lined roads and, for this reason, were, unfortunately, quite often confused with those hiding in the shadows of the trees; but in order to insure that the divisive dissatisfaction this had caused in many segments of the population would be avoided in the future, the new law was passed and ratified as quickly as possible and herewith goes immediately into effect; people who comply will have no further reason for dissatisfaction, those who do not comply, however, will continue to suffer the consequences of breaking the law. Where it is necessary to walk through

forests and along tree-lined roads because there is no open countryside yet and the traffic routes have trees beside them, the roads will be precisely designated and specified; personnel will be posted at the beginning and end of each forest lane or tree-lined road and, if the road is very long, at stations along the way; any number of inspections can be undertaken, whose technical and statistical data will serve the republic for the general improvement of the social conditions in the land and, in so doing, are desirable.

Where the forests begin, tables are set up, stakes driven into the meadows, wooden surfaces put on top; whoever wishes to walk through the forest goes to one of the tables, where an official standing behind the table or sitting on a tree stump hands him two forms which are to be filled out and handed over for examination before starting the journey; both forms are then signed, one is stuck in a file, the other is to be taken along and handed over to the other official at the end of the woods. Both forms, differently colored, contain the following, identical questions, which are to be answered truthfully:

NUMBER _____

SERIAL NUMBER _____

DATE _____

TIME _____

NAME _____

DATE OF BIRTH AND PLACE OF BIRTH _____

OCCUPATION _____

PREVIOUS OCCUPATIONS IF APPLICABLE _____

_____

PLACE OF RESIDENCE _____

PREVIOUS PLACES OF RESIDENCE IF APPLICABLE _____

_____

ADDRESS _____

PREVIOUS ADDRESSES IF APPLICABLE _____

WHICH OCCUPATIONS DID YOU PURSUE IN WHICH PLACES OF RESIDENCE _____

_____

NAME, DATE OF BIRTH, PLACE OF BIRTH, OCCUPATION, PREVIOUS OCCUPATIONS IF APPLICABLE,

PLACE OF RESIDENCE, PREVIOUS PLACES OF RESIDENCE IF APPLICABLE, ADDRESS, PREVIOUS ADDRESSES IF APPLICABLE OF YOUR FATHER, OF YOUR MOTHER, OF YOUR BROTHER(S) AND SISTER(S), OF YOUR WIFE, OF YOUR CHILDREN, OF YOUR EMPLOYER, OF YOUR FAMILY PHYSICIAN, OF THE EMPLOYER OF YOUR FATHER, OF THE EMPLOYER OF YOUR MOTHER, OF THE EMPLOYER OR EMPLOYERS OF YOUR BROTHER(S) AND SISTER(S), OF THE EMPLOYER OF YOUR WIFE, OF THE EMPLOYER OR EMPLOYERS OF YOUR WORKING CHILDREN IF APPLICABLE, OF YOUR FATHER-IN-LAW, OF YOUR MOTHER-IN-LAW, OF YOUR BROTHERS-IN-LAW, OF YOUR SISTERS-IN-LAW, OF THE BROTHER(S) AND SISTER(S) OF YOUR FATHER, OF THE BROTHER(S) AND SISTER(S) OF YOUR MOTHER, OF THE BROTHER(S) AND SISTER(S) OF YOUR FATHER-IN-LAW, OF THE BROTHER(S) AND SISTER(S) OF YOUR MOTHER-IN-LAW, OF THE CHILDREN OF THE BROTHER(S) AND SISTER(S) OF YOUR FATHER, OF THE CHILDREN OF THE BROTHER(S) AND SISTER(S) OF YOUR MOTHER, OF THE CHILDREN OF YOUR BROTHER(S) AND SISTER(S), OF THE CHILDREN OF THE BROTHER(S) AND SISTER(S) OF YOUR WIFE, OF THE CHILDREN OF THE BROTHER(S) AND SISTER(S) OF YOUR FATHER-IN-LAW, OF THE CHILDREN OF THE BROTHER(S) AND SISTER(S) OF YOUR MOTHER-IN-LAW, OF YOUR POSSIBLE SECOND WIFE, OF THE BROTHER(S) AND SISTER(S) OF YOUR POSSIBLE SECOND WIFE, OF THE CHILDREN OF THE BROTHER(S) AND SISTER(S) OF YOUR POSSIBLE SECOND WIFE, OF YOUR POSSIBLE SECOND FATHER-IN-LAW, OF YOUR POSSIBLE SECOND MOTHER-IN-LAW, OF THE BROTHER(S) AND SISTER(S) OF YOUR POSSIBLE SECOND FATHER-IN-LAW, OF THE BROTHER(S) AND SISTER(S) OF YOUR POSSIBLE SECOND MOTHER-IN-LAW, OF THE CHILDREN OF THE BROTHER(S) AND SISTER(S) OF YOUR POSSIBLE SECOND FATHER-IN-LAW, OF THE CHILDREN OF THE BROTHER(S) AND SISTER(S) OF YOUR POSSIBLE SECOND MOTHER-IN-LAW, OF YOUR POSSIBLE THIRD AND OF EVERY OTHER POSSIBLE WIFE AND HER IMMEDIATE RELATIVES AND OF ALL EMPLOYERS AND FAMILY PHYSICIANS OF THOSE NAMED AND THEIR CLOSE RELATIVES AND ACQUAINTANCES AND OF ALL RELATIVES AND ACQUAINTANCES OF THEIR EMPLOYERS AND FAMILY PHYSICIANS NOT LISTED HERE _____

_____

_____

_____

_____

_____

_____

_____

_____

_____

_____

_____

_____

_____

_____

_____

_____

_____

_____

_____

_____

_____

_____

_____

_____

_____

_____

_____

_____

_____

_____

_____

_____

_____

_____

_____

_____

_____

_____

_____

ARE YOU AND ALL PERSONS LISTED BY YOU SATISFIED WITH YOUR EMPLOYER (YOUR EMPLOYERS)

AND FAMILY PHYSICIAN (FAMILY PHYSICIANS) _____

_____

_____

_____

WHERE ARE YOU GOING _____

WHAT DO YOU WANT THERE _____

WHY DON'T YOU WANT TO GO SOMEWHERE ELSE _____

_____

WHY DON'T YOU STAY HOME IN THE FIRST PLACE _____

_____

WHEN DO YOU EXPECT TO ARRIVE WHERE YOU ARE GOING _____

WHERE WILL YOU STAY THERE _____

WHEN WILL YOU COME BACK _____

WILL YOU COME BACK AT ALL _____

WHY _____

WHY NOT _____

HOW MUCH MONEY DO YOU HAVE WITH YOU _____

HOW MUCH MONEY ARE YOU BRINGING ALONG IN ADDITION TO THAT WHICH YOU ARE NOT LIST-

ING HERE _____

WHY DON'T YOU WANT TO LIST HERE THE MONEY WHICH YOU ARE BRINGING ALONG IN ADDI-

TION BUT ARE NOT LISTING HERE _____

_____

FOR WHAT DO YOU NEED THE MONEY THAT YOU HAVE WITH YOU _____

_____

IS IT YOUR INTENTION TO MAKE PURCHASES AT YOUR DESTINATION OR ALONG THE WAY ____

_____

WHY _____

WHEN _____

WHERE _____

FROM WHOM _____

WHAT DO YOU WANT TO BUY _____

_____

DO YOU ALSO WANT TO BUY ANYTHING ELSE WHICH YOU ARE NOT, HOWEVER, LISTING HERE

_____

WHAT _____

WHY _____

WHEN _____

WHERE _____

FROM WHOM _____

WHY DON'T YOU WANT TO LIST HERE WHAT ELSE YOU ARE BUYING BUT NOT LISTING HERE

_____

WHAT ARE YOUR MONTHLY EARNINGS _____

HOW MUCH DO YOU PAY IN TAXES _____

HAVE YOU EVADED TAXES IN RECENT TIMES _____

WHY _____

WHEN _____

FOR HOW MUCH DID YOU DEFRAUD THE STATE _____

HOW FAST DO YOU WALK _____

DO YOU WANT TO REST ALONG THE WAY _____

WHY _____

WHEN, WHERE, AND HOW OFTEN _____

HOW TALL ARE YOU _____

HOW MUCH DO YOU WEIGH _____

HOW LONG ARE YOUR FEET _____

LENGTH OF YOUR STRIDES _____

DO YOU FAVOR THE INTRODUCTION OF GENERAL TESTING FOR SEXUALLY TRANSMITTED DIS-

EASES _____

ARE YOU AWARE THAT YOU ARE A BAD PERSON THROUGH AND THROUGH _____

OR ARE YOU BY ANY CHANCE OF A DIFFERENT OPINION _____

ARE YOU HAPPY IN YOUR OCCUPATION _____

WOULD YOU RATHER TAKE UP ANOTHER OCCUPATION _____

WHICH _____

WHY _____

WOULDN'T YOU LIKE TO BECOME A W O O D C U T T E R _____

_____

OR WOULD YOU RATHER FIND EMPLOYMENT IN ANOTHER BRANCH OF THE LUMBER INDUSTRY

_____

ARE YOU BY ANY CHANCE SUFFERING FROM VENEREAL DISEASE _____

DO YOU HAVE GONORRHEA, SYPHILIS OR SOFT CHANCRE _____

ARE YOU UNDER TREATMENT _____

DETAILS ABOUT THE INDIVIDUAL WHO STUCK YOU WITH THE VENEREAL DISEASE _____

_____

ARE YOU UNEMPLOYED _____

WHY _____

DO YOU LIKE FORESTS _____

WHY _____

DO YOU LIKE TREE-LINED ROADS _____

WHY _____

DO YOU LIKE TREES IN GENERAL _____

WHY _____

DO YOU REGARD TREES STANDING ALONE OR IN GROUPS AS ADVANTAGEOUS, DISADVANTA-
GEOUS, OR DANGEROUS _____

_____

WHY _____

HAVE YOU ANSWERED ALL QUESTIONS TRUTHFULLY _____

HAVE YOU ANSWERED SOME QUESTIONS FALSELY _____

WHICH _____

WHY _____

WHICH QUESTIONS THAT YOU AREN'T LISTING HERE DID YOU ANSWER FALSELY_____

_____

WHY _____

WHY DON'T YOU WANT TO LIST HERE THOSE QUESTIONS WHICH YOU ANSWERED FALSELY BUT
AREN'T LISTING HERE THAT YOU ANSWERED THEM FALSELY_____

_____

WHY DON'T YOU WANT TO LIST HERE THOSE QUESTIONS WHICH YOU ANSWERED FALSELY BUT
AREN'T LISTING HERE THAT YOU ANSWERED THEM FALSELY BUT AREN'T LISTING THAT HERE____

_____

OTHER _____

FURTHER NOTATIONS _____

NOTATIONS BY THE AUTHORIZED OFFICIAL _____

_____

REMARKS BY THE AUTHORIZED OFFICIAL _____

SIGNATURE OF THE AUTHORIZED OFFICIAL _____

SIGNATURE OF THE AUTHORIZED OFFICIAL _____

SIGNATURE _____

SIGNATURE _____

DATE _____

TIME _____

SERIAL NUMBER _____

Before starting the journey the two forms are to be filled out, handed over
to the official for inspection and examination; both are signed by him, he
sticks one in a file, the other is to be taken along and handed over to the

agent at the end of the forest road.

Individuals who do not fill out the forms truthfully must pay a fine not to exceed the number in today's date in local currency; for illiterates, there are clerks appointed who sit on tree stumps, hold typewriters in their laps, listen to the dictation of the applicants, and fill out the documents.

If you should meet an authorized official in the forest along the way, you have to let him examine the form you brought along, answer his questions genially, truthfully, joyfully, and without excuses.

At the end of the woods the latter form is to be handed over to the agent there.

On the part of the authorities, everything is being done to protect the population from the black men hiding in the shadows of the trees. Despite the new regulation, the population is called upon to be wary, even while traveling on monitored forest roads, because it is suspected that now the black shadows of the trees are disguising themselves in counterfeit or stolen uniforms and molesting, threatening, reviling, abusing, and insulting the people.

Parents and those qualified to teach are urged not to let their children and pupils forget the game WHO IS AFRAID OF THE BLACK MAN in the shadows of the forest.

Prior to the time of the new law, many are said to have disappeared in the forests without a trace. Among executive authorities, where there was no explanation for it, the speculation was offered that the black shadows of the trees and everything that was hidden in them were to blame. However, after the time of the new law many people or even more than before are said to have still disappeared in the forests without a trace. Members of the judiciary offered the speculation that only the shadows of the trees are to blame, which now disguise themselves in counterfeit or stolen uniforms and make fools of the law-abiding population.

But voices were also heard to say that those who disappeared in the forests were actually arrested by the executive authorities because statements taken from their forms indicated that they hide behind trees. People who made such claims are later said to have been reported missing in the forests without a trace or else identified, arrested, locked up as members of the forest's shadows and turned over to the courts by agents.

Who are these black men anyway? Do they live in the shadows of the trees or disguise themselves with the darkness of the forests, or how do they so easily portray the twilight in the tree-lined roads? It is reported by the judiciary that these questions can only be answered when the menace is completely eliminated because only thereafter, based on statistical, criminal, philosophical, psychological, mathematical, economical, historical, biological, physical, zoological, medical, psychotherapeutical, botanical, paleontological, parapsychological, chemical, cybernetical, archaeological, sociological, logical, and many other studies, which, of course, are continually under way, but which can only be evaluated, judged, edited, scrutinized, checked, controlled, and classified after the elimination of the menace, can these questions be answered in a way that everyone will be able to understand.

Many, who at first speculated publicly that there were n o black men at all but supposed they were only the i n v e n t i o n of higher authorities and also a carefully planned pretext under which to justify the new law and its effects and consequences, and much more, because in reality there are only the shadows of the trees, in which no one and nothing can any longer hide, are said to have afterwards disappeared in the forests without a trace or else were identified, arrested, locked up, and turned over to the courts by agents on the basis of their black shadows.

According to higher authorities, there are plans to soon disclose new measures of even greater effectiveness:

the intention is to cut down all forests, tree-lined roads, and, if necessary, fell trees standing alone in the countryside,

because

1. one wishes, once and for all, to rid the population of the threat of the shadows behind the trees as well as those dark elements hiding in them, which then would no longer have any places to hide because there would be no more trees behind which they could hide,

2. should the practical enforcement of the new law become difficult because there are not enough agents available, the aforementioned plan would make enforcing the new law unnecessary,

3. the high rate of unemployment, which exists everywhere in the land and is steadily increasing, thereby would be eliminated by training and hiring all do-nothings as woodcutters or employing them in other branches of wood

processing, because the l u m b e r i n d u s t r y would record a b o o m like none before, because then m u c h m o r e w o o d t h a n e v e r would be available for processing.

The huge supply of wood which will suddenly build up will be utilized to produce,

in a d v a n c e ,

barn floors, barns, bay windows, beams, beaters, beds, benches, boards, bolts, bowls, bridges, buoys, carts, chair backs, chairs, chests, closets, coffins, cots, crates, doors, fences, flutes, footbridges, footstools, forks, gallows, gates, halls, houses, huts, lattices, mats, mills, plates, poles, rafts, rings, roofs, shingles, ships, skiffs, slats, spoons, staircases, stalls, steps, sticks, stools, swings, tables, trunks, walls, wheels,

paper,

anterooms, bedrooms, beer coasters, border crossing gates, bunk beds, chalets, charcoal, customs barriers, dance floors, dining rooms, door frames, door latches, dung pits, floating hotels, gymnasiums, horizontal bars, living rooms, log cabins, matches, piers, playpens, rafters, railroad crossing gates, road barriers, saltshakers, school benches, school compasses, sideboards, slides, table legs, toilet seats, tree supports, wheelbarrows,

artificial limbs, balconies, counting houses, credenzas, figures, hinges, parquets, portals, racks, railings, scaffoldings, trays,

ax handles, baby carriages, birdhouses, book bindings, broomsticks, children's rooms, children's toys, clothes hooks, clothes trees, corridors, doghouses, gangplanks, hinge pegs, hop poles, knife handles, labor camps, nesting boxes, pepper shakers, plank floors, rack wagons, rocking chairs, rocking horses, scarecrows, shovel handles, storerooms, street barriers, window frames, wastepaper baskets, warning signs, traffic signs,

cubbyholes, vestibules,

bar ornaments, bookshelves, butter churns, obstacle courses, paprika shakers, pickax handles, radio tables, toy guns, weekend homes,

granaries, paneling, seats of government,

guillotines,

ceiling structures, inn furnishings, lamp shade frames, screwdriver handles, canal pile planking,

carpentry workshops, telegraph poles,
playground apparatus, riverbank reinforcements,
bay windows in seaports,
bridges for prospective streets,
bay windows for women looking down,
bridges for prospective rivers,
bridges for prospective canals,
scarecrows for prospective nurseries,
bridges for prospective streets across prospective streams, rivers, canals,
waterways, ravines and the railings bordering them, footbridges across prospective ravines for the prospective necessity of the prospective elimination
of the prospective interruption of prospective mountain pasture paths for
prospective foxes, chamois, hares, stags, chickens, dogs, cats, horses, deer,
cattle, sheep, weasels, nanny goats, squirrels, ibexes, skunks, giraffes, cam-
els, antelopes, dromedaries, elephants, water buffaloes,
and much more;
the wood still leftover will then be stained with tallow or tarred, kept in
storerooms protected from rain, hailstones, snowfall, humidity, and other
harmful weather conditions;
but there are also many who say t h e   w h o l e   l a n d   w i l l   p r o b-
a b l y   v e r y   s o o n   b e   d e c o r a t e d   a n d
p a n e l e d w i t h w o o d .

every step will be a signal knock beneath the grains and knotholes of
the wooden boards mounted on top of the ground you will hear
streams rivers and waterfalls rushing between the cracks of the planks
later trodden down the water of the marshes will rise seep in and the
cotton grass will creep upwards

careful planning and the incorporation of cybernetics will guarantee the
economic boom in the land,

the marsh marigold will climb up out of knotholes

you see the billposters still traveling through the land, the metal fittings on their knapsacks glisten in the air, their hammers strike the barn walls; log cabins are being built in clearings for the agents, bunk beds for the soldiers; you hear the stakes pushing into the grass, the orders of the higher officials, the sounds of the typewriters among the shrubs,

>   blueberry pickers startled herbalists chased away
>   blackberry gatherers plunge from rock ledges

throughout the forests you hear the chopping of the axes, which are leaned against the trunks during the noon break; perhaps fall is coming, yes, that's quite possible,

fall is coming,
one fears chestnuts and other fruits that fall from trees,
to guard against that one holds his hand above his head or wears a wide-brimmed hat;
snipers in trees and hedges have it harder, they are discovered more easily.

The Village Square

—The village square is empty; except for the well in the center, there is nothing in the village square.
—You're right, the village square is empty.
—We can walk across the village square,
I said. We had hidden in the blacksmith's workshop, cheeks pressed up against the walls; no one saw us, and you said
—let's walk across the village square then, the village square is empty.

No, that's not right, that's a lie, because the doors of the houses are opening up, all the door wings are swung aside, the hinges creak; hoses are being tossed out of the open doors, water hoses, hoses with nozzles; the window wings are also being opened; I see hoses falling out of the windows, too, out of those on the second floors, then also out of those on the third; hoses are already connected to all the water faucets; to the houses which have no water faucets, no running water in the rooms, hoses are led from those houses which do have them; the whole village is riddled with hoses, fire hoses, for every wall of every house at least one hose, if not two; torches are being made ready, leaned against the walls, in case something should come in the night.

Yes, I remember the night, heard the steps of those on guard. They carried lights in front of them, whistled songs and listened for sounds in the sky, walked through the narrow streets, stopped every once in a while, set their lanterns on the ground, yawned loudly or softly, *tired, rest, listen, sleep, rather, like to, no, watch out, have to, tired, rest.*

Yes, I remember the night, many years ago, when the birds plunged down out of the darkness for the first time; we were lying in the kitchen in front of the stove, seeing the last flame flicker out, observing the embers getting dimmer and dimmer; through the crack of the stove door that couldn't be closed all the way, we saw the black lines slowly splitting, breaking up, the bits of embers crumbling and dissolving into cinder clumps. Then a faint singing and shrieking in the black air came through the window from the outside. Then we heard a peculiar scratching in the walls, and the singing was waiting outside, screaming in front of the door; we wrapped ourselves in our blankets, lying on the floor, pulled the coarse, skin-abrading cloth around our ears; but the screaming stayed there, it kept on singing outside for quite a long time. Then the next day everybody saw what had happened, looked into the eye sockets in the pecked-blind mortar of the walls of the crumbling, seriously injured houses.

Last night, however, everything was quiet; in the morning those on guard went to the mayor and reported to him

—*Mister Mayor, the darkness remained calm, the air silently still.*

A few people are lowering a long fire hose down into the well, getting a hand pump, connecting it to the hose, in order to let water shoot up with a lot of pressure from the interior of the planet.

I can hear a peculiar, faint, high-pitched singing in the air, similar to far-off swarms of mosquitoes, getting louder, coming closer; the people have grabbed their hoses, aiming the hose nozzles at the walls; the singing in the screaming air, soon it will be directly over us and will swoop down from above the roofs of our houses right past our heads, the screaming in the softly buzzing, trembling, singing light.

And the first ones fall out of the sky, clawing themselves into the walls, but the water faucets have already been turned on, too; somebody next to the well pushes the lever of the hand pump up and down like mad, working up a sweat; one can see only a strident fluttering darting through the loudly singing airwaves, and detect a transparent beating of wings in the trembling bel canto of the horned roaring light, being sung completely off-key in irregular ascending and descending chromatic patterns, surging through the valleys of audible wave crests in between countless claws poised to dig in at any time or the keenly honed, razor-sharp, open scissors of their beaks; the whole atmosphere seems to be filled with them; one can barely detect their bodies; only when a somewhat dense part of a flock has clawed into a piece of the wall, because just at that moment no water is being sprayed there, do I see, or think I see, on the one hand, a completely white, on the other hand, a rather colorless, not-quite-transparent, nearly penetrated-by-sunbeams plumage, with wings letting the light through as if made of glass feathers, which are shimmering nervously and beating about wildly;

(sometimes the thought enters my mind that these birds are not really flying in the air, but, more likely, in the light, using the currents that encircle the planet along with the ascending and descending lightning surges of the waterfall-like sunray cataracts crashing up and down, and using the last shimmers of every dusk to glide over it, their wings following in the wake of a warm wind of light along the course of the far-traveling, draining away sunset rays);

while their beaks peck around in the mortar uncontrolledly, hysterically, uninhibitedly, quite violently knocking out the wall, as if it were the flesh of their prey that it has just taken every bit of their strength to attack one more time; and these birds, to be sure, on the one hand, peck like woodpeckers at the worms in a tree trunk, on the other hand, peck a lot faster; more than twice as fast, or from three to ten times as fast, are these mortar hackers, wall peckers, whose beaks, however, don't peck at any worms, because there aren't any in concrete; inconceivable; although one shouldn't be all that certain when facing such an incredibility; and, if one day someone suddenly were to come upon a wall with mortar maggots or concrete wall beetles, which, perhaps, then would have their little galleries, shafts, lanes running in lines and winding through the interior of houses like wood beetles in old furniture or trees, such things wouldn't surprise me anymore; because, when, after years of the most exhaustingly hard work, we've finally managed to clear most of our forests, forcing the several surviving insect species, because of a lack of wood, to undergo a change in their diet, as well as in their way of life and their habits, or else die out, then I would certainly expect that, after a period of time, some robust wood beetle or species of wood worm, for example, instead of staying inside the no-longer-available tree trunks or furniture, would be able to move into the concrete of bridges and houses, to crawl around as they construct their many-branched system of galleries as densely as possible, without it being obvious or noticeable, until one day in the future, let's say, for example, a brand new bridge spanning a river, out of the clear blue sky appears to have been hit by lightning, collapses, caves in, perhaps right during rush hour, because the galleries of the wood beetles that had been retrained as lime worms or mortar beetles, wood worms, have spread so extensively, almost completely hollowing out the entire inner soul of a supposedly hypothetical bridge, so that its collapse could not have been prevented; but there are no such animals yet, which might cause our houses and bridges to collapse, no insect species, no worms that live in the lime interior of the walls and build galleries, lanes, which then could be pecked out of the walls by the mortar peckers; but how these birds do peck into the lime, hacking at it and ripping out whole chunks of houses, swallowing them through their beaks down their gullets to their crops, and doing so without any indication of trying beforehand to make a wall-chunk bite smaller, but immediately devouring them with ravenous hunger to be able to start pecking again right away; woodpeckers do not suggest even a faint comparison, much too slow; with what speed these wall peckers or lime-knocking peckers know how to neatly peck absolutely everything out of all the joints between the bricks, and how they have adapted the camouflage colors of their plumage to the daylight air; and when we see their dangerous, razor-blade-sharp, quick beak scissors, we should be mindful of our good fortune that these creatures in the daylight-colored feathers are not stalking carnivores tracking any living prey, because when such flocks appear in the thousands or even many more, no living visible being could show itself on the surface of the landscape without being at once surrounded by a diving flock, and in minutes being chopped to pieces and devoured, because when one sees how they constantly sharpen their quick beak scissors right after using them by the prolonged, careful rubbing of both beak halves against each other, they can easily not only peck the lime mortar out of all the wall joints to let it soon thereafter disappear into the gullet's crop of their invisible throat, but also, while flying over long distances, they can easily cut up or tear up or chew up every difficult-to-cross light wall of the horizon's ravines and every air grating or air railing, no matter how high, in the rugged regions where access is restricted during bad weather, and that's why every flight path and its continuation had always been essentially assured; these piranhas of our pinstripe-patterned airship cathedrals.

Everywhere in the village there is steady spraying from the calibers of all available hoses, starting with thin garden hoses and graduating to the thickness and length of professional fire department hoses; there is a hissing from all water mains and out of all water pipes, out of the complete diapason of the waterworks organ; the walls are already quite wet or damp, but at least not one of these fowl is getting into even the most hidden of cracks in the lime mortar; the panic of the flock every time it is touched by one of the water jets; unfortunately, one cannot even suggest an explanation for what causes this, but that is not important now, would not be of lifesaving significance; but now, all of a sudden, through the earth's skin and through the rocky ground of the thick-skinned foothill ridges, louder than it has been for a long while, as if on its hidden surface an underground, innerplanetary thunderstorm contest is reaching its climax, seeking a decision, you hear the ocean water table, which, admittedly, we had not plundered and exploited to such an extent for a long time, an unexplored, never before seen by anyone, only presumed to exist, underground fresh water ocean begins to rush and roar, rolling around in itself, somewhat ominously murmuring, as if gasping out of high mountain interfoldings, somewhat like smashing and grinding throughout, and now becoming obvious that it is grumbling and rebelling, because, while its level was dropping on account of our presumably enormous water consumption at that time, one or perhaps several of its subterranean side lakes and secondary lagoons had probably changed into rivers and gushing mountain streams escaping, flowing away through the inner galleries of the planet, down through and beneath the regions neighboring ours, crossing them underneath in their barren beauty or beautiful barrenness, flowing down into a desert or steppe that may have been completely hollowed out in its interior, there to remain deposited a long time, awaiting the metamorphic ages for transforming into an artesian well, which explodes out of the earth, blasting through the planet's skin, being spewed into the atmosphere or spewing itself upwards into the eternal, fair-weather sky of an everlasting desert or steppe, up into a sky that is nearly burning; but before being charred, with the speed of a nameless hurricane, it flees along an extensive piece of land, spreading over part of the continent and filling its air-columned halls to the bursting point, forcing the wind to glide upward into one of the already opened entrance halls to its dressing room, almost across the sea, to first display above the shore of the approaching coast, beach arches, domes, and vaults, darkening the firmament's stuccowork ceiling of heaving masses of cumulus clouds anchored in the atmosphere; and for the climax of the horizon's opening performance a well-orchestrated thunderstorm including every available theatrical thunderclap retrieved from the entire collection of stage properties from all well-known, unknown, and forgotten weather theaters, the retouched effects of dramatic art used in the most impressive, most advantageous, and most promising application of the artistic principles governing the unleashing of nature; all the countries and countrysides that will fit within the generous embrace of its farthest arches fill the vaulted auditorium of our continental theatrical institution to capacity, so that, sold out from the orchestra of its lowlands with their underground garages up to the balconies of its iced-in glacier-tongued galleries, it bursts and explodes, so that, after sinking back down, sinking in for a long time, it rests in one of the oceans' dormitories for the performance of the coming millennium; or else, more simply and much closer, less indirectly, it sprays right up at us, and is quickly spread over the walls of the houses and huts of the village.

The mountain springs are rushing, the man next to the well is still pumping fiercely, *spray 'em down,* one of them shouts, *aim, that's right, water, more, up there, pecks lime, that's the way, come, there, eats the wall, keep goin', go at 'em, faster, everything else is indecent, backs mortar, no way to behave, just let 'em stay hungry, nobody gives us anything, spray 'em down.*

Until all birds are successfully driven away from the houses; little plaster is destroyed, hardly worth mentioning; the mayor watches from the open window of the magistrate's office on the second floor of the town hall; a stray water jet hits him in the face, while below the man with the hose is trying to chase a bird away from the lime mortar of the windowsill; the mayor wipes his face with his sleeve.

Gradually the animals give up, rise into the sky, gather into a flock farther above; only now and then the singing, wind-flapping wings in the much quieter, only hoarsely shrieking air, gliding up with the wind, accompanied by the ebbing away song of the softly and easily whistling light, whose shrill sound weakens in the distance, is disappearing, or has already disappeared, or has disappeared behind the torn curtains of a just-completed day's work; the flock, too, is lifting higher and higher above the roofs, its fog-veiled, wing-flapping bird cloud, of which only the blinking opening and closing tips of the beaks are visible, which zip by the thousands like small, oblong, black-and-yellow-bordered semicolons or inverted semicolons through the expansive networks of paneled ceilings in the firmament, as if pesky, unpleasant winged insects had nested in the creases of its sunray-furrowed, leathery skin, under the not-very-well-taken-care-of, rather neglected, but quite splendid head of hair in the horizon's social lion's cage, out of whose tarry, slightly moldy-smelling, wooden bathing cabin walls, emerges only a faint hum, like that of a thick mosquito swarm, or else a far-off, barely audible buzzing; no, now it is the cry of all nights that has risen from the glistening sand banks of the already quite calmly flowing away afternoon, still glowing faintly into and out of the rushing river's main channels through the creaking mill wheels of the nerve-racking, noisy sun, opening up, spreading over the incalculable ceiling of the parachute sky, whose decorative strips are artistically nailed and doweled into the airy, light ray-geared cupola of coming and going days behind the next world; it sinks back into the impenetrable, networked delta of the gray of dawns and dusks into the rising river's main current of one night, in whose waves it one day reaches an unknown, generally kept-secret ocean; and, surrendering in its surf, you may now forget everything that I wrote here so that you could remember it well.

The water faucets have been turned off; the man next to the well has stopped pumping, wipes the sweat from his face with his sleeve. The mayor closes the window on the second floor of the town hall, disappears into the darkness of the magistrate's office. The people laugh at each other, breathe easier, some embrace, others sigh with exhaustion from the past excitement, *done, finally, got through it, well done, off the hook again, without a hitch, were lucky, nice job, good work, showed them again, won't come back too soon, driven away, scared away, chased away.*

The hoses are rolled up again, they're stored in the houses, the hand pump next to the well is carried away, the people slowly withdraw, want to rest, the door wings clap shut, the window wings are unfolded, ready for the house's departure into a dream, the teacher goes to the inn, the priest takes the village chronicle from the shelf and begins to write.

Later on they might set up the benches again, but some have also expressed the wish to leave the benches out on the meadow on the edge of the village, *nicer, grass, wind, more greenery, flowers, quiet, view, air on a meadow.*

—*The village square is empty; except for the well in the center, there is nothing in the village square.*
—*You're right, the village square is empty.*
—*We can walk across the village square.*

We had hidden in the blacksmith's workshop, cheeks pressed up against the walls; no one saw us, and you said
—*let's walk across the village square.*

We then walked across the village square. No one saw us. Even far behind us and long after that, the square remained empty. The people had gone to bed, fallen asleep. The walls, darkened and damp, began to cover the village with a decreasingly transparent, grayly tinged skin, which slid outward from the attics as if it had been stored in every attic on thick, boltlike rolls, wound up on clothes drying racks perhaps, or on winches or similar devices expressly made for it, possibly to be automatically machine operated, too, one never knows for sure, which must have always stood at the ready behind the skylights in the roof framework below the windows, from where the grayly tinged skins usually made their exit from the roof, outside to join with other patches of skin pushing outward from neighboring roof frameworks and skylights, to grow together or stick together with them, although not very neatly, because, in addition, the seams or joints showed bulges or some thickening here and there, almost like tied sausage gut; when the skin patches were out of all the skylights, they were joined together to form a single skin, which then rose above all the gables like a gigantic rotten rain skin hovering widely over the whole village, slightly arched, almost vaulted, curving upwards over the houses; as you looked into the sky then, you thought that over this vicinity the sky displayed rather oddly appealing air bulges between carelessly or somewhat sloppily knotted twilight ends, especially over the dark wet walls; and, in passing, one might have thought that twilight hadn't sunk down from the sky onto the houses, as it usually does, but the reverse, it must have been blown, atomized out of the house walls, the houses, out of the chimneys, also escaping up out of the cellar windows, out of the depths of the pantries and bins heaped with coal; much too early on this afternoon, mist steamed out of the cracks and gaps of the very dark, wet walls of this much too early late afternoon, on which the paving stones were still wet from the defensive water spraying maneuvers against the destructive members and inhabitants of a hostile atmosphere and its merciless sky, which thoughtlessly and without consideration excretes everything it can no longer hold virtually onto our heads or into our hair, at best, tossing it at our feet, or sinking it into the inner universe of our eyes so that, for everything that we subsequently see, the original breadth of our view is from then on as good as blocked, eliminated from the outset. The sun, having broken out, begins to draw the moisture out of the lime mortar; the stone slabs are dried by the wind.

The village square is still empty.

Outlook

They talk a lot about blue rocks and horses. Gradually, this region is turning into a spilled paint box.

In the same atmosphere,
                         in the same time period
(or else different and or else not),
it is possible and quite permissible
to wrap the village in white or colored wrapping paper with or without a
company label
                 or to fold it up into an ellipsoid with the dimensions of a con-
ventional rugby ball,
                    to throw it over one of your shoulders
                    or through one of your armpits ten or more or fewer
meters
        behind your back,
to make a turn into another region.

Afterword

Austrian writer Gert Jonke is one unmistakable voice on the contemporary German literary scene. While he has written poetry, dramas, radio plays, and film scripts, the strength of his reputation rests mainly on his works of fiction.[1] Their rich language, inventive humor, and compelling form combine to provoke a critical awareness of the problematic interrelationship of language, reality, and art.

Born in 1946, the son of a pianist and a builder of musical instruments, Jonke was raised in Klagenfurt in southern Austria by his mother. As a boy he studied piano under her tutelage. He became interested in writing poetry in his teenage years, when he discovered that in free verse a world of limitless expressive opportunity was open to his exploration. Following service in the Austrian Army, he enrolled in the School for Film and Television of the Academy for Music and Arts in Vienna but, after several semesters' attendance, left without graduating. He has been a free-lance writer since 1969.

Early in his career Jonke found support for his creative endeavors in the *Forum Stadtpark* in Graz, that enclave of the avant-garde in Austria named for their meeting place in a city park. The Graz group comprised a diversity of progressive literary and artistic talents linked by their impatience with conventional themes and techniques and their aim to illustrate the complexity of reality by antitraditional and experimental means.[2] Jonke made a successful literary debut at the age of twenty-three and has been the recipient of many stipends and literary honors. He was the first writer to be awarded the prestigious Ingeborg Bachmann Prize, given him in 1977.

Intermittently, the author has lived for extended periods outside Austria, residing at length in Berlin and London; and he has traveled widely, including South America and the Orient in his itineraries. He now makes his home in Vienna and Klagenfurt.

The German text of *Geometrischer Heimatroman* (*Geometric Regional Novel*) is available in two versions. The first, published by the Suhrkamp Verlag of Frankfurt am Main,[3] stirred lively discussion in literary circles when it appeared in 1969. Critics referred to its young author as the creator of a modern topographical regional novel[4] and a significant contributor to Austria's emergence as a force in experimental literature.[5] In 1980 a second version was published by the Residenz Verlag of Salzburg in his omnibus *Die erste Reise zum unerforschten Grund des stillen Horizonts* (The First Journey to the Undiscovered Bottom of the Quiet Horizon). Jonke explained in the preface to the collection that his intention had been to make relatively modest revisions of earlier works, restoring passages that in hindsight he wished had not been deleted, and eliminating certain passages which should not have been included. However, the process came to involve more extensive rewriting than initially anticipated, as well as the addition of some totally new material. In a subsequent interview, the author recommended that those works be read in their revised form,[6] and it is the 1980 version of *Geometrischer Heimatroman* that has been translated here. Many of the changes made in it are stylistic refinements, occasionally affecting no more than a word or two on a page, although very few pages were left untouched. On the other hand, Jonke substantially revised the elements of the narrative which bolt into surrealism, notably the descriptions of savage attacks by incomprehensible birds, a purported threat from shadowy figures who live in the forests, concrete parasites, a paranoid woodcarver, and an underground ocean's role in a meteorological theatrical performance.

Geometric Regional Novel makes no concessions to easy reading. Its author's unique method—constantly interrupting the narrative thread with the introduction of new strands, playing with time and logic, maintaining a relentless tentativeness, and describing ordinary things in such extraordinary detail or from so many different perspectives that they become exceedingly difficult to recognize—places unusual demands upon readers by continually misleading their expectations and denying them the comfort of fiction's customary guideposts.

The title itself gives an indication of the author's antitraditional posture. The literary genre designation *Heimatroman* is usually rendered as "regional novel." However, the element *Heimat* in the German compound is culturally charged. Often translated as "homeland," it is a word that implies notions of security and belonging, rootedness in the soil, and participation in the shared values of the rural community. The *Heimatroman,* as advocated by writers of regional fiction at the turn of this century, celebrated the simple agrarian life, the native language or regional dialect, and the natural landscape; but it was also inclined to display a certain provincial narrowness and to exaggerate the idealization of rural life in contrast to life in the alienating, hostile metropolis. The setting, typically, was the village or a single farm, which stood for the intact, harmonious society. Features of the surrounding landscape, such as mountains or dense forests, often helped guarantee its isolation. A patriarchal landowner or other sympathetically portrayed characters conveyed the society's conservative values; but, as they tended not to intellectualize or reveal their inner selves, an omniscient narrator sometimes interpreted meaning while giving realistic accounts of events over significant periods of time. Any disturbance of the existing order was commonly the result either of a natural calamity or of someone crossing the boundary of this closed system to enter or leave it. Foreigners who intruded brought catastrophe upon the community; similarly, the native inhabitant who left this secure realm met with misfortune.[7]

Not surprisingly, since the genre's emphasis on hearth, home, and exclusivity lent itself well to their nationalistic impulses, the regional novel was exploited as a propaganda tool by the Third Reich. During the 1950s and 1960s, moviemakers employed the traditional regional literature's themes in the *Heimatfilm* of the German cinema. And today these themes remain the standard fare of popular novels.

Many writers of Jonke's generation failed to see the distinctions drawn earlier between urban living and country living; in light of contemporary social reality, these lacked authenticity.[8] They sought to expose rural life to be just as brutal as life in the city, if not more so. It was in this context that Jonke wrote his regional novel. The incongruity in attaching the adjective *geometric* to the genre signals his rejection of the assumptions upon which that literary form was based and his opposition to outmoded principles of style, language, and plot. He radically transforms the regional novel through experimentation with its conventions and parody of its traditional elements.

Beyond its ironic function in the title, the word *geometric* is an apt reference to the predominant method of description. The narrative provides limited information about an agrarian village and its inhabitants, most of it being presented in terms of exact spatial dimensions and relationships. For instance, the mountain range north of the village is shaped like "a sine curve, a cosine curve, and a sine and a cosine curve, each displaced by one and three-quarter phases" (9). Pasture fences divide the countryside into rectangles. Tree stumps along the edges of the village square are circles of a specific diameter. Even the leaves of the trees do not fall and scatter haphazardly but are "precisely distributed" (15) over the square by the wind. The emphasis accorded outlines, surfaces, and sensations of sight and sound is part of an effort to mediate a physiologically discerned world without regard for feelings or opinions. Paradoxically, the world reduced to geometric expressions seems less, not more, real.

When this technique is used to describe people it dehumanizes them. Thus, in daily life—whether they are visiting each other, lining up on the square, mixing mortar, or disciplining their children—the villagers' actions look methodically habitual. Repetition in the text of truncated, wooden sentence structures and minutely detailed descriptions of body movements help convey the automatonlike quality of their behavior. When the bridgekeepers want to communicate with each other across the river, "They stand upright on the banks of the river with legs spread thirty degrees, raise their hands with elbows angled, and cup their hands, wrists and palms, and closed fingers to form a hollow, open cylinder around their wide-open lips" (34). The human element is so diminished on this geometrically articulated landscape that objects assume a level of dominance vis-à-vis people. The caption beneath a diagram of the village square maintains that the object world dictates patterns to the human world (41), and the powerful influence of patterns—of routines, traditions, repetition, but especially of linguistic patterns—is evident in the lives of the villagers.

Despite a preponderance of Austrian artifacts, dialect, and characteristics, the setting is not Austrian particularly, the incidence of exotic impressions precluding a strictly Central European locale. Rather, the rural village can be viewed as an abstraction of a rigid, preindustrial society facing the onslaught of rampant development, exploitation, and bureaucratization. Mathematical description, the reduction of characters to types or faceless, interchangeable figures, and multiple permutations made in a few basic situations and elements support a view of the village as a structural model and of interactions among the inhabitants as functions of that system.

In the preindustrial condition, the village's most prominent figures are the teacher, mayor, and priest, here portrayed as parodies of the regional novel's traditional characters. The teacher is depicted as the prime inculcator of societal values, but his lessons are pedantic and the moralistic rules of conduct he imparts to his pupils become comically trivial admonishments. Overall, his litany of prescribed and proscribed behaviors has a sinister implication: utter subordination of the individual to the system. The local priest and the affable but possibly feebleminded mayor are figures who appear preoccupied with observing ceremony and keeping records while remaining indifferent to constructive social involvement. By default, they perpetuate the status quo. Other members of the community, such as the café owner and the blacksmith, perform roles identical to those of the generations who preceded them. That nearly every aspect of village life has been codified in some way is suggested by the intrusive presence of warnings, instructions, aphorisms, diagrams, historical records, ordinances, and forms.

Eventually, provisions of a law passed under the pretext of protecting citizens from "black men" who hide in the shadows of trees enable all activity in the region to be monitored and controlled by a nebulous, increasingly repressive higher authority. At that point, simply to take a walk in the woods requires submission in duplicate of a lengthy application (six pages in the text) listing not just pertinent vital statistics, but also irrelevant and even self-incriminating data about the petitioner, as well as information about all his near and distant relatives and acquaintances. Questions of the type, "Why don't you want to list here what else you are buying but not listing here?" (101) draw the hypothetical applicant into a linguistic quagmire. The law, riddled with speciousness and duplicity, elevates legal obfuscation to the level of absurdity. This is one of many instances of parody of the language of government, of science, or of the press that accounts for much of the book's humor.

Jonke is not one to articulate social criticism explicitly. Instead, he makes visible the process by which bureaucracy and official regimentation insidiously pervade society. His antipathy to authoritarianism in any guise and to unthinking patterns of behavior and language emerges from the text's obsession for narrative equivocation. Nothing in the prose can be taken for granted because every assertion is somehow countered or made questionable and all literary illusion is exposed to a destructive scrutiny.

Traditional considerations of plot have been cast aside in favor of an episodic structure that sets sketches of particular village situations next to fantastic, dreamlike interludes or documentary inserts. The twenty-one essentially self-contained text segments, and sometimes parts within them, challenge linearity and logic; they give an impression of having been assembled randomly, as one might put together the pieces of a puzzle. This effect also stems from there being no characters who perform the conventional function of moving the action forward. The figures who come closest to providing a connective thread are the "I" and "you" narrators who want to cross the village square. Nevertheless, when the event that has been anticipated throughout the novel finally occurs and the two observers do cross the square, the novel ends. That their action leads to no other outcome relates to the narrative focus, which is not on actual events but on the infinite range of possible events.

Another disorienting feature is that narrative levels shift frequently, resulting in an intriguing web of patterns and layers. The "I" and "you" of "The Village Square" chapters are anonymous eyewitnesses, reporting the action without reflecting upon it. Yet, although both are observing the village square from the same vantage point in the blacksmith shop, they contradict each other's statements in formularized dialogue, a circumstance which casts doubt upon their reliability and distances them from the reader. The acknowledgement that they are in hiding and do not want to be seen further reduces their credibility. In other sections of the book, however, the narrator is well informed about the village's history and institutions, seems to have participated in events, and indulges in speculation about the future, while ambiguous references to "you" may be addressing the reader. In yet other passages, where the "i" narrator is apparently recalling past events, those "flashbacks" are set apart from the rest of the text by their indented margins, the absence of capital letters and punctuation, and occasionally by being printed in italics.

The characteristics of rumor and hearsay prevail, amplified by a heavy reliance on the subjunctive mood and frequent use of the word *or*. Rather than furnish a ready-made perspective on events, the narrative tentatively offers multiple points of view, but no single one is put forward as being of greater validity than any other; all are equal in rank. Even the blueprintlike diagrams that have been included do not serve the purpose of clarification; they merely duplicate information already supplied in writing. Uncertainty is cumulative in the account of a performance in the village square by a tightrope walker. From the outset, it is apparent the event is being described at second hand because it is related as indirect discourse. The passage also contains fragments of the audience's comments on the show; their opinions differ markedly, essentially nullifying each other. The discrepancies in their assessments indicate that the relationship between what people perceive and what actually happens is dubious, at best. This point is made even more forcefully by the local art critic's comprehensive but blatantly subjective review of the show, which is simultaneously amusing and disturbing. The review's lofty treatment of and exaggerated praise for what is basically a carnival act and its exploitation of the event for political purposes show that language, instead of mirroring reality objectively, imposes particular values and attitudes on its users. Although the narrator's aloof and totally nonjudgmental reporting affords a strong contrast to the art critic's biased account, on balance it is no more informative.

The high point of the performance, the concluding act, has a wholly unpredictable outcome. During the artist's tightrope walk, a tree limb to which his rope is attached breaks and the rope gives way. Some eyewitnesses report seeing him climbing up into the sky and disappearing, while others observe him fall toward the well in the center of the square, breaking his back over the well winch. Ironically, the art critic reserves his highest accolades for the precision with which the backbone cracks exactly in the middle but fails to acknowledge the artist's death.

The case can be made that the story of the tightrope walker is a parable for the experience of the writer, whose delicate balancing act consists in pursuing an infinite vision in art and still remaining accessible to an audience. Elsewhere, Jonke has described the self-imposed challenge in his writing as daring to stretch the limits of sensation, feeling, and thinking to the point where one teeters on the brink of insanity.[9] While that challenge has serious implications, he is inclined to treat them with humor and wit.

If there is no reliable point of view in this work, time as a formal element is likewise ambiguous. To be sure, the passage of time is evident from alterations in the landscape, especially in the changing images of the trees growing, being cut down, their trunks being dug up, benches being installed where trees once stood, and benches being removed to make way for combat with the enigmatic birds. But there is an obvious disparity between that time frame and the time spent by the two narrators who observe these changes while they are waiting for an opportunity to cross the village square unobserved. Time appears to be slowed down whenever the author extends the instant of perception to be able to supply exhaustively detailed description of an object, but it is just as likely to be speeded up to make perceptible the growing of tree branches. The narrative also tests the possibilities for time to move, not just forward, but backward or in a circle. The various treatments of time, viewed as narrative adaptations of film techniques, lend a cinematic quality to the prose. Time hypothetically marches in reverse in the narrated encounter of a hiker with a bull, as each element of the incident is repeated backward in the negative and the story annuls itself by revising the original premise. For the reader who becomes absorbed in the details of the first part, the surprising realization that an opposite version is equally plausible induces self-conscious laughter. The bull episode occurs early in the book and gives a clear indication of the author's intention to undermine one's certitude of expectations.

The unwavering tentativeness in this experimental narrative helps illuminate Jonke's impulse to explore the connection between experience and the language used to express experience. He often employs a series of related or synonymous terms where a single word would customarily suffice, insinuating that individual words have been devalued in common usage. The process of accumulation is a means of restoring their original scope and power, thereby reinvigorating language. His concern about the relationship between reality and its portrayal aligns Jonke with the concrete poets, and he participates in their endeavor to create by linguistic manipulation an aesthetic entity that stands for itself, rather than represents an exterior reality.[10] Exhibiting a concretist preference for condensation and asyntactical structure, he sometimes dismantles conventional language, reassembling the components into a design that carries its own meaning, a practice in effect in the following passage, where the lines render visually the gradually diminishing audibility of the hissing sound:

... then i believed having heard another hissing in the air

fur

button

wedge

which rolled down the other side of the hill behind us

hair

window

wood

moving farther and farther away. . . (23)

Language thus released from the constraints of longstanding practice is free to manifest its verbal, visual, and acoustic richness.[11] At the same time, it requires the reader to contemplate the text as an object, whose configuration and transmission of meaning are interdependent. In another example reiterated many times in a single chapter, the three-line pattern:

the old blacksmith,
his wife
and his son, the present blacksmith (50)

designates the family unit, its members having identity only in a collective sense, not as individuals, interchangeably carrying on monotonous routines.

In consequence of their significance, every effort has been made in the translation to preserve the visual characteristics of the original text. These include spaces on the printed page which may indicate time gaps or pauses, lapses of memory, or space in the physical world; variations in typography which help to differentiate levels of discourse; the content of signs and excerpts from official documents printed in capital letters to more closely approximate their actual appearance; and the expansion of certain words or phrases for emphasis.

Several of the narrative devices employed by Jonke—narration by an anonymous persona who articulates a purely surface reality, mathematically precise description, reduced characters, nonlinear progression, adaptation of cinematic practices—are among techniques advanced for the *nouveau roman* by Alain Robbe-Grillet.[12] But Jonke uses them experimentally, not necessarily as a proponent of the *nouveau roman;* and it may be that some of the techniques are imitated with the intent to parody them. At times, for example, common things and simple processes are described in such provocative detail that they appear totally unfamiliar, as if the eye were too close to properly focus.[13] The section "Corrugated Iron and Door" evinces one ramification of this distorted perspective; namely, reflections or shadows cannot be differentiated from the actual object. The blurring of distinctions between what is objective and what is subjective is the precondition that enables language to leap into fantasy.

Language's creative power is the central issue in the description of the birds who periodically invade the village, which Jonke expanded considerably for the revised version. The birds, a hitherto unknown species whose attacks are completely unpredictable, represent a random occurrence in an otherwise controlled mathematical system. For this reason, their description stands in marked contrast to the meticulously observed topography of the village. Initially, the flock's gradual advancement is experienced synesthetically as a "softly buzzing, trembling, singing light" (110). As the menacing flock increases in strength and proximity, the language used to describe it gathers momentum correspondingly. By the accretion of modifiers and dependent clauses, single sentences expand in a linguistic crescendo to fill one or more pages of text, until both the described phenomenon and the description itself seem beyond comprehension and ultimately overwhelming.

Contributing to the potency of the language are its richly complex comparative linkages. They create effects that well exceed the usual parameters of metaphor. Elaborating on the sources of the water being used to hose birds down from walls, an artesian well blasting through the earth's crust is invested with thunderstorm characteristics and imaginatively associated with a continental weather theater, which, "sold out from the orchestra of its lowlands with their underground garages up to the balconies of its iced-in glacier-tongued galleries, . . . bursts and explodes . . ." (114). The original text includes a number of the gigantic word clusters for which Jonke's writing is well known. The coining of compound words is a German language feature that has no equivalent in English. Necessarily, I have rendered many of Jonke's word combinations as phrases or genitive constructions. In the description of the meteorological theater, for example, "wolkenballungshaufenherumschiebende Firmamentstukkaturdeckenbearbeitung" in the original is translated as "the firmament's stuccowork ceiling of heaving masses of cumulus clouds" (114); and a reference to the voracious birds, "diese Piranhas unserer nadelstreifgemusterten Atmosphärenschiffskathedralen," is rendered as, "these piranhas of our pinstripe-patterned airship cathedrals" (113). The coined words augment the expansiveness of the narrative by their exaggerated proportions and suggest a range of potential interrelationships among their constituent elements. Yet, never one to be heavy-handed, Jonke tempers the linguistic intensity of the passage by interweaving it with playfully whimsical images and idiosyncratic logic. His speculation on the evolution of mortar maggots, for instance, does not seem too farfetched if one can first accept the scenario of a world devoid of trees and thus unable to accommodate certain worms and insects in their normal habitat. At the end, he counters the foregoing labyrinthine explanation, as if it were all in jest, with an ironically simple alternative.

Whether one is inclined to agree with scholarly assessments of *Geometric Regional Novel* as either an exemplar of postmodern regional literature or strictly an experimental text,[14] its significance is enhanced when one considers how the work may have anticipated the current serious interest in hypertext fiction created on the computer. Comparisons can be drawn between Jonke's prose and hypertext's interactive features, branching options, expansive networks of textual components, graphic elements, and use of font changes and documentation.[15]

In the end, reality in Jonke's model is too complex and, at the same time, too seamless to be expressed by means of ordinary conceptual thought and traditional literary structures. Thus, his narrative looks skeptically upon efforts to articulate the experience of the world, a stance underscored in its open-ended conclusion. *Geometric Regional Novel* eschews definitive utterance in favor of a multiplicity of indeterminate discourses, made all the more absorbing by their rich language and comic elements. Free of authorial domination, its readers are in the position of collaborators in creating the literary work, obliged to seek out patterns or correspondences among the narrative fragments, to configure and reconfigure the textual components on their own terms.

Johannes W. Vazulik
United States Military Academy
July 1999

NOTES

[1]For a discussion of Jonke's major works, see my "An Introduction to the Prose Narratives of Gert Jonke," *Major Figures of Contemporary Austrian Literature,* ed. Donald G. Daviau (New York: Lang, 1987), 293-311, and my "Gert F. Jonke," *Dictionary of Literary Biography,* vol. 85 (1989).

[2]For a discussion of the *Forum Stadtpark Graz,* see Hilde Spiel, *Austrian Literature after 1945* (New York: Austrian Institute, n.d.), 13-20.

[3]Excerpts have been published in translation as *"Geometric Regional Novel*/Excerpts," trans. Johannes W. Vazulik, in *Dimension: Contemporary German Arts and Letters,* 8 (1975): 222-41. An unpublished translation of the complete work is available in my "G. F. Jonke's *Geometrischer Heimatroman:* Translation and Critical Introduction," Ph.D. diss., Case Western Reserve, 1974.

[4]Siegfried Schober, "Immer stimmt irgend etwas nicht," *Süddeutsche Zeitung* (Munich), 31 May 1969, 7.

[5]Hannes Rieser, "Die Grammatik des Dorfes," *Literatur und Kritik* 5 (1970): 560-66.

[6]Andrea Kunne, "Gespräch mit Gert Jonke," *Deutsche Bücher* 4 (1983): 255-6.

[7]For more detailed discussion of the genre, see Andrea Kunne, *Heimat im Roman: Last oder Lust?* (Amsterdam: Rodopi, 1991), 23-40, and Karlheinz Rossbacher, *Heimatkunstbewegung und Heimatroman* (Stuttgart: Klett, 1975), 137-242.

[8]See Michael Wegener, "Die Heimat und die Dichtkunst," *Trivialliteratur,* ed. G. Schmidt-Henkel, et al. (Berlin: Literarisches Colloquium, 1964), 53-64.

[9]Kunne, "Gespräch," 253.

[10]See Liselotte Gumpel, *"Concrete" Poetry from East and West Germany* (New Haven: Yale University Press, 1976), 10.

[11]See Gumpel, 56.

[12]Alain Robbe-Grillet, *"Snapshots" and "Toward a New Novel,"* trans. Barbara Wright (London: Calder, 1965), 54-57, 59-65, 92-93.

[13]See Kunne, "Gespräch," 255.

[14]For a discussion of postmodern characteristics in *Geometrischer Heimatroman,* see Kunne, *Heimat im Roman,* 201-32; for an assessment of the work as an experimental text, see, e.g., Wolfgang Düsing, "Avantgardistische Experimente mit einer konservativen Gattung: Gert Jonkes *Geometrischer Heimatroman,*" in *Wesen und Wandel der Heimatliteratur,* ed. Karl Konrad Polheim (Bern: Lang, 1989), 87-103.

[15]For a discussion of hypertext possibilities, see Robert Coover, "The End of Books," *New York Times Book Review,* 21 June 1992, 1, 23-25.

DALKEY ARCHIVE PAPERBACKS

PIERRE ALBERT-BIROT, *Grabinoulor.*
YUZ ALESHKOVSKY, *Kangaroo.*
FELIPE ALFAU, *Chromos.*
  Locos.
  Sentimental Songs.
ALAN ANSEN,
  Contact Highs: Selected Poems 1957-1987.
DJUNA BARNES, *Ladies Almanack.*
  Ryder.
JOHN BARTH, *LETTERS.*
  Sabbatical.
AUGUSTO ROA BASTOS, *I the Supreme.*
ANDREI BITOV, *Pushkin House.*
ROGER BOYLAN, *Killoyle.*
CHRISTINE BROOKE-ROSE, *Amalgamemnon.*
GERALD BURNS, *Shorter Poems.*
GABRIELLE BURTON, *Heartbreak Hotel.*
MICHEL BUTOR,
  Portrait of the Artist as a Young Ape.
JULIETA CAMPOS,
  The Fear of Losing Eurydice.
ANNE CARSON, *Eros the Bittersweet.*
LOUIS-FERDINAND CÉLINE, *Castle to Castle.*
  London Bridge.
  North.
  Rigadoon.
HUGO CHARTERIS, *The Tide Is Right.*
JEROME CHARYN, *The Tar Baby.*
MARC CHOLODENKO, *Mordechai Schamz.*
EMILY HOLMES COLEMAN,
  The Shutter of Snow.
ROBERT COOVER, *A Night at the Movies.*
STANLEY CRAWFORD,
  Some Instructions to My Wife.
RENÉ CREVEL, *Putting My Foot in It.*
RALPH CUSACK, *Cadenza.*
SUSAN DAITCH, *Storytown.*
PETER DIMOCK,
  A Short Rhetoric for Leaving the Family.
COLEMAN DOWELL, *Island People.*
  Too Much Flesh and Jabez.
RIKKI DUCORNET, *The Complete Butcher's Tales.*
  The Fountains of Neptune.
  The Jade Cabinet.
  Phosphor in Dreamland.
  The Stain.
WILLIAM EASTLAKE, *Castle Keep.*
  Lyric of the Circle Heart.
STANLEY ELKIN, *Boswell: A Modern Comedy.*

Criers and Kibitzers, Kibitzers and Criers.
  The Dick Gibson Show.
  The MacGuffin.
ANNIE ERNAUX, *Cleaned Out.*
LAUREN FAIRBANKS, *Muzzle Thyself.*
  Sister Carrie.
LESLIE A. FIEDLER,
  Love and Death in the American Novel.
RONALD FIRBANK, *Complete Short Stories.*
FORD MADOX FORD, *The March of Literature.*
JANICE GALLOWAY, *Foreign Parts.*
  The Trick Is to Keep Breathing.
WILLIAM H. GASS, *The Tunnel.*
  Willie Masters' Lonesome Wife.
ETIENNE GILSON, *The Arts of the Beautiful.*
C. S. GISCOMBE, *Giscome Road.*
  Here.
KAREN ELIZABETH GORDON, *The Red Shoes.*
PATRICK GRAINVILLE, *The Cave of Heaven.*
GEOFFREY GREEN, ET AL, *The Vineland Papers.*
JIŘÍ GRUŠA, *The Questionnaire.*
JOHN HAWKES, *Whistlejacket.*
ALDOUS HUXLEY, *Antic Hay.*
  Point Counter Point.
  Those Barren Leaves.
  Time Must Have a Stop.
GERT JONKE, *Geometric Regional Novel.*
TADEUSZ KONWICKI, *A Minor Apocalypse.*
  The Polish Complex.
ELAINE KRAF, *The Princess of 72nd Street.*
EWA KURYLUK, *Century 21.*
DEBORAH LEVY, *Billy and Girl.*
JOSÉ LEZAMA LIMA, *Paradiso.*
OSMAN LINS, *The Queen of the Prisons of Greece.*
ALF MAC LOCHLAINN,
  The Corpus in the Library.
  Out of Focus.
D. KEITH MANO, *Take Five.*
BEN MARCUS, *The Age of Wire and String.*
WALLACE MARKFIELD, *Teitlebaum's Window.*
DAVID MARKSON, *Collected Poems.*
  Reader's Block.
  Springer's Progress.
  Wittgenstein's Mistress.
CARL R. MARTIN, *Genii Over Salzburg.*
CAROLE MASO, *AVA.*
HARRY MATHEWS, *Cigarettes.*
  The Conversions.
  The Journalist.

Visit our website: www.dalkeyarchive.com

DALKEY ARCHIVE PAPERBACKS

Singular Pleasures.
The Sinking of the Odradek Stadium.
Tlooth.
20 Lines a Day.
JOSEPH McELROY, *Women and Men.*
ROBERT L. McLAUGHLIN, ED.,
    Innovations: An Anthology of Modern &
      Contemporary Fiction.
JAMES MERRILL, *The (Diblos) Notebook.*
STEVEN MILLHAUSER, *The Barnum Museum.*
    In the Penny Arcade.
OLIVE MOORE, *Spleen.*
STEVEN MOORE, *Ronald Firbank: An Annotated*
    Bibliography of Secondary Materials.
NICHOLAS MOSLEY, *Accident.*
    Assassins.
    Children of Darkness and Light.
    Hopeful Monsters.
    Imago Bird.
    Impossible Object.
    Judith.
    Natalie Natalia.
    Serpent.
WARREN F. MOTTE, JR., *Oulipo.*
YVES NAVARRE, *Our Share of Time.*
WILFRIDO D. NOLLEDO, *But for the Lovers.*
FLANN O'BRIEN, *At Swim-Two-Birds.*
    The Best of Myles.
    The Dalkey Archive.
    Further Cuttings.
    The Hard Life.
    The Poor Mouth.
    The Third Policeman.
CLAUDE OLLIER, *The Mise-en-Scène.*
FERNANDO DEL PASO, *Palinuro of Mexico.*
RAYMOND QUENEAU, *The Last Days.*
    Odile.
    Pierrot Mon Ami.
    Saint Glinglin.
ISHMAEL REED, *The Free-Lance Pallbearers.*
    The Last Days of Louisiana Red.
    The Terrible Threes.
    The Terrible Twos.
    Yellow Back Radio Broke-Down.
REYOUNG, *Unbabbling.*
JULIÁN RÍOS, *Poundemonium.*

JACQUES ROUBAUD, *The Great Fire of London.*
    The Plurality of Worlds of Lewis.
    The Princess Hoppy.
    Some Thing Black.
LEON S. ROUDIEZ, *French Fiction Revisited.*
SEVERO SARDUY, *Cobra & Maitreya.*
ARNO SCHMIDT, *Collected Stories.*
    Nobodaddy's Children.
CHRISTINE SCHUTT, *Nightwork.*
JUNE AKERS SEESE,
    Is This What Other Women Feel, Too?
    What Waiting Really Means.
VIKTOR SHKLOVSKY, *Theory of Prose.*
JOSEF SKVORECKY,
    The Engineer of Human Souls.
CLAUDE SIMON, *The Invitation.*
GILBERT SORRENTINO, *Aberration of Starlight.*
    Crystal Vision.
    Imaginative Qualities of Actual Things.
    Mulligan Stew.
    Pack of Lies.
    The Sky Changes.
    Splendide-Hôtel.
    Steelwork.
    Under the Shadow.
W. M. SPACKMAN, *The Complete Fiction.*
GERTRUDE STEIN, *Lucy Church Amiably*
    The Making of Americans.
    A Novel of Thank You.
PIOTR SZEWC, *Annihilation.*
ALEXANDER THEROUX, *The Lollipop Trollops.*
ESTHER TUSQUETS, *Stranded.*
LUISA VALENZUELA, *He Who Searches.*
PAUL WEST,
    Words for a Deaf Daughter and *Gala.*
CURTIS WHITE,
    Memories of My Father Watching TV.
    Monstrous Possibility.
DIANE WILLIAMS,
    Excitability: Selected Stories.
DOUGLAS WOOLF, *Wall to Wall.*
PHILIP WYLIE, *Generation of Vipers.*
MARGUERITE YOUNG, *Angel in the Forest.*
    Miss MacIntosh, My Darling.
LOUIS ZUKOFSKY, *Collected Fiction.*
SCOTT ZWIREN, *God Head.*

Visit our website: www.dalkeyarchive.com

Dalkey Archive Press
ISU Campus Box 4241, Normal, IL 61790–4241
fax (309) 438–7422